EDMUND+OCTAVIA

THE
DULCIE CHAMBERS
MYSTERIES

BY KERRY J CHARLES

AN EXHIBIT OF MADNESS
(PREVIOUS TITLE: PORTRAIT OF A MURDER)

FROM THE MURKY DEEP

THE FRAGILE FLOWER

A MIND WITHIN

LAST OF THE VINTAGE

THE HAND THAT FEEDS YOU

THE HAND THAT FEEDS YOU

A Dulcie Chambers Mystery

Kerry J Charles

EDMUND+OCTAVIA

This book is a work of fiction. Names, characters, places, and incidents either are products of the author's imagination or are used fictitiously. Any resemblance to actual events or locales or persons, living or dead, is entirely coincidental.

Cover Image: *Die Falknerin*, 1880, Hans Makart.
This image is in the public domain.

ISBN-13: 978-0-9963393-6-0

Edmund+Octavia Publishing, Falmouth, Maine, USA

For Mum
(See… I was paying attention!)

CONTENTS

When you look at art made by other people,
you see what you need to see in it.
~ Alberto Giacometti

CHAPTER ONE

One would think, watching the hawk soaring over the trees, arched wings spread wide, that the bird was loyal. It flew up high, spiraling on the thermals, then slowly slid back down, coming to an immediate halt on the woman's arm. A piece of raw meat was on the heavy leather glove that covered her hand. With lightening precision the bird snatched it away. It continued to sit on her arm, eyeing its surroundings warily.

The woman spoke to the hawk in a steady, quiet voice as she walked along. Not a soothing voice. More of a decisive, instructive one. Yet still low and soft and rhythmic. The hawk flapped its wings, but its claws retained their firm grip on the stiff leather. The woman moved into a clearing and motioned her arm up. The hawk spread its wings again, flapping them hard, this time pulling away into flight. It circled twice, then landed on a nearby tree branch, watching the woman.

One would think, as a casual observer, that the hawk was loyal to its mistress.

One would be wrong.

Esmerelda Graves knew better. She had trained too many hawks to believe for one instant that they had any loyalty at all to her. They were, in fact, loyal to one thing only: their insatiable desire for meat. She provided a ready source but had to be careful. Feed them too much, and they would become complacent. They wouldn't perform. Feed them too little and they would look elsewhere for a meal. She had learned that the hard way early on, losing two of her best birds to the wilds.

Each morning Esmerelda carefully weighed her seven birds, one by one. She calculated exactly how much meat each should receive. Then she planned her training for them accordingly. Today she worked with Mordred. She referred to him as Mordred the Handful. She kept the leather jess firmly tethered to one of his legs so that she could wrap it through her fingers quickly and keep him on her arm. He often flapped his strong wings against the strap, trying to escape. Earlier in the year he had even pecked at her arm once. The sharp, hooked beak had easily cut through her nylon jacket, sinking into her skin beneath. It had been a learning experience for her. She knew just how far she could push him, just how long she could hold him captive before allowing him to take flight again. Each bird had its own distinctive personality like that.

Esmerelda watched Mordred as he perched up in the tree. He was motionless, his golden-brown eyes with black, piercing pupils intently fixated on a particular spot in the clearing. She walked over to it and began scuffing her rubber boots around on the ground. The smell of rotting wood and humus, along with a cloud of tiny twig bits and dried leaf fragments, wafted up from the ground.

From the corner of her eye Esmerelda watched Mordred. She knew what was coming. Suddenly, the hawk swooped down from the tree, and within a split-second plucked a mouse from beneath the dried leaves, then carried it back up to the branch where he began feasting on it. Esmerelda had never even seen the small creature. She rarely did. But she had known it was there - Mordred always knew where they were hiding.

❧

"You've decorated this office quite tastefully." It wasn't a complement, but a commentary on what Vanessa Rich thought was an overly lavish setup. She maneuvered her somewhat large frame behind Dulcie's desk, crowding behind Dulcie's chair so that she had to slide it in further to make room. She was now effectively pinned against her desk, craning her neck around to see what Vanessa was doing. Vanessa was looking more closely at a painting hanging on the wall behind Dulcie. It was an original Winslow Homer watercolor.

The true intent of Vanessa's comment was not lost. "That's a gift," Dulcie replied. "From a close personal friend," she continued, instantly regretting the additional information.

Vanessa wheeled around quickly and, over the top of her wire-rimmed glasses, stared down at Dulcie. In the crowded space she was uncomfortably close. Dulcie was still twisted around, her neck now hurting from the awkward position. "Is it really?" Vanessa said. "Must be quite a well-off friend. I'm assuming that this is original and not some cheap knock-off."

Dulcie took a deep breath. '*Stay calm,*' she willed herself. "Yes, it is original. And yes, my friend was," she said, forcing a smile.

"Waaaas?" interjected Vanessa, stringing out the word into a long, questioning syllable.

"He died and left the painting to me," Dulcie stated bluntly.

"Ah, yes. I remember hearing something about that," Vanessa said, shaking her head. The implication was clear – she believed that Dulcie had used what was politely referred to as her *feminine wiles* to gain favor with a certain gentleman before his untimely death. It wasn't true of course. The relationship had been solely professional and based on a mutual interest in the arts. '*If I were a man,*' Dulcie thought, '*Would the same assumption be made?*' She knew the answer. No, it would not.

The friend in question had been the former chairman of the Maine Museum of Art's board of directors, the position that Vanessa Rich now held. She had been elected as such only the week before but had made her presence felt immediately. She walked back around Dulcie's desk and continued to survey the room. Dulcie eased her chair back and rubbed her neck.

"I suppose that one can stay then," Vanessa said, jerking her head in the direction of the Homer. "But we'll need to replace some of these things with less expensive alternatives." She rapped the antique oak desk with her hefty knuckles. The large diamond and ruby rings on her fingers flashed in a ray of sunlight that had just glinted in from the window. "I think you'll find that we need to be running a tighter ship around here." She looked directly at Dulcie with cold, blue eyes. "I'm afraid that the museum will not be able to continue accommodating the style to which you've become accustomed."

Dulcie inhaled slowly but said nothing.

Vanessa took one last look around the room, eyeing the tall mahogany armoire in the corner that served as Dulcie's coat closet. "Hmpf," the large woman snorted, then marched out the door closing it firmly behind her.

The room was silent. Dulcie sat back in her chair, rubbing her neck again. Then she heard a soft tapping on the door.

"Yes?" she said, annoyance edging into her voice.

Rachel opened the door a crack and peeked around it. "Is it safe to come in?"

Dulcie groaned and nodded. Rachel slid inside and closed the door again behind her. The untamable red curls on her head bounced as she walked across the room and sank into the chair opposite Dulcie's desk.

Dulcie looked over at her. "Rachel, what are we going to do?" she asked, knowing the question was completely rhetorical.

Rachel grinned. "We're going to do our best to avoid that woman at all costs," she said.

"That's just it!" Dulcie exclaimed. "The woman is focused entirely on costs! She wants to replace all of the furniture in here with... well, I don't know what with, but certainly something much cheaper."

"How's that going to help?" Rachel asked, glancing around the room. "Is she planning on selling all of this?"

"I have no idea. And it was probably just some kind of power-play bluff to intimidate me." Dulcie's head was beginning to ache now along with her neck.

"Has she?" asked Rachel.

Dulcie looked up from rubbing her temples. "Certainly not!" she replied.

"Well then," Rachel continued. "I suggest we just go about doing what we've always been doing, which is running a museum. With one small exception."

"What's that?" asked Dulcie.

"Try to stay one step ahead of *Cruella de Vil*," she replied.

Dulcie laughed, in spite of herself. "You're right, as always. This is why I pay you so well," she said.

"Ah, but don't let Cruella know," Rachel countered.

As Dulcie's assistant, Rachel was the calm, organized force behind each tiny detail of Dulcie's work. Without Rachel, as Dulcie had said many times, she couldn't function. It was an exaggeration of course. Dulcie would certainly be able to function, she would just have a far more difficult time, not to mention putting in many more long hours.

Rachel was well aware of this, and equally aware that her position was well compensated. She could never do Dulcie's job, nor did she want to. Rachel was quite happy to work behind the scenes making sure that everything was done correctly. She was a perfectionist and like all perfectionists she often sought perfection simply for perfection's sake. At times it drove Dulcie nuts.

Rachel stood and glanced out the window. "Do you think she's gone yet?" She hoped to see Vanessa's large frame departing down the sidewalk. No such luck.

"She's never gone. She'll always be looming somewhere," Dulcie answered gloomily.

"Oooh, here's something to perk you up!" Rachel said, ignoring her boss and leaning closer toward the window. Her forehead bumped on the glass. "That handsome boyfriend of yours! Looks like he's coming to visit!"

Dulcie instantly sat up straight and smoothed back her dark hair.

"That got your attention!" Rachel quipped. "I'll leave you to him!" She glided across the Persian carpet that covered most of the hardwood floor and opened the door. Winking at Dulcie, Rachel disappeared, leaving the door open.

Dulcie looked at the carpet, then over at the armoire. Was her office lavish? She'd never even pondered the question. She hadn't actually decorated it herself. Well, she had rearranged the furniture, but she hadn't added anything except the Winslow Homer painting. Her predecessor had somehow acquired the furnishings. Dulcie had never considered that they were excessive – they seemed appropriate given that she often met with wealthy donors and high-ranking associates in the art world. They would expect a certain level of décor. Cheap office furniture might make them question how the museum was operating or whether Dulcie and her staff took proper care of the irreplaceable works of art that filled the building.

Her thoughts were interrupted by a shadow in the doorway and the sound of someone clearing his throat. "You were miles away," he said.

"Nick, you have no idea how glad I am to see you!" Dulcie greeted him.

"I hope that's always the case and not just in response to recent company," Nick replied. He unzipped his leather jacket, walked across the room and sat in the chair that Rachel had just vacated.

Dulcie looked at him quizzically.

"Rachel briefly filled me in," he added in response.

"Ah, yes," Dulcie stated flatly. She leaned back in her chair once again. "Nick, what am I going to do?"

Nick thought for a moment. "The first thing you're going to do is close your computer and get your coat."

Dulcie glanced at her watch. It was well after five. Her stomach rumbled. "Does this mean you're taking me somewhere fabulous?" she asked, wiggling her eyebrows.

Nick stood and fished her coat out of the armoire. "I'm taking you somewhere," he said. "Fabulous might be pushing it."

Dulcie allowed him to slide her coat over her shoulders, then steer her out of the office.

They swept by Rachel at the front desk. "Night, Rachel!" Dulcie called back to her. "We're going someplace fabulous!" She heard Rachel groan behind her.

A warm spring breeze wafted down the street as Nick held the door open for Dulcie. The nights were still chilly, but the days were growing longer and warming up considerably. After the brutal winter they'd just suffered through, the change was welcome. Dulcie felt almost giddy as they strolled down the brick sidewalk.

"So where are we going?" she asked.

"Actually, I don't know," Nick said. "Feel like chowder?"

"Perfect," Dulcie answered. There was one place to go for that: Gilberts. They crossed one of Portland's uneven cobblestone streets, and continued along, following the waterfront. Several seagulls were squawking loudly on the sidewalk, fighting over a few French fries that someone had dropped.

"Rats with wings," Dulcie quipped. "That's what my Dad always said."

"Very true," Nick agreed. "Funny how they're so iconic. You see the tourists feeding them, taking pictures... if they only knew." He shook his head and shooed the birds away so that he and Dulcie could get into the restaurant door.

Dulcie scanned the room, half expecting to see her brother. Gilberts was a favorite haunt.

"See Dan?" Nick asked.

Dulcie smiled. "Am I that predictable?" she asked.

"No, but he is," Nick answered. He pulled out a chair for her at an empty table.

They were barely seated when the door opened again, and Dan came in. Nick glanced at Dulcie. "See what I mean?" he said.

Dan spotted them and sauntered across the room. "Hey! Not interrupting an intimate dinner for two, am I?" He pulled up a chair, not waiting for an answer.

Dulcie laughed. Gilbert's wasn't exactly an intimate place. Beer, chowder, batter-covered clams in cardboard boxes, these were the staples of the menu. The lights were always on brightly and the smell of fried seafood permeated the air. It was coastal Maine's version of comfort food.

Dan waved to the waitress across the room. She tossed her blonde hair over her shoulders, grinned at him and hurried over. Dulcie laughed under her breath. "Service is never that quick for me," she muttered.

"Can't help my natural charms," Dan replied.

Nick chuckled without looking up from the menu.

"What'll ya have?" the waitress asked.

"I'll start with a beer, please," Dulcie said. She pointed to one on the menu.

"Me too," both men chorused.

The waitress giggled and took their order. Dan watched her walk away, hips swaying a bit more than Dulcie had seen before.

"So Dan," Nick said, pulling Dan's attention back to the table. "Business picking up with the warm weather?"

"A little," he replied. "Not quite the tourist season yet. The boat's ready though. I installed a refrigerator unit over the winter. Did Dulcie tell you? No more coolers skidding across the deck!" Dan's Casco Bay touring business was in its fifth year and prospering, especially with Dulcie investing as a silent partner. "How about you?" Dan asked. "Any good cases?"

Nick shook his head as their beer arrived at the table. "Pretty routine at this point. A couple of thefts. A possible arson. Someone's missing a boat. That kind of stuff."

"Exciting," Dan quipped.

"I, on the other hand," interjected Dulcie, "Now have the distinct pleasure of working for *Cruella de Vil*."

Dan put down his beer and looked pointedly at his sister. "Is this the new board chair?" he asked.

"It is," she said. "And she has made her presence known immediately. Already, I can't stand her."

Dan picked up his beer again and gave her a mock toast. "I have to hand it to you, Dulcie. I'm the one who deals with the crazy public all day, but you seem to get more of the, shall we say, *distinct* personalities."

"She does seem to have the market cornered on that," Nick added. "What's the backstory on this one?"

Dulcie uttered an exasperated sigh. "Kind of the usual. Wealthy, of course. Bossy. Opinionated. Thinks she knows exactly how to run a museum even though she never has before in her life."

"What's she done for work? How'd she get rich?" Dan asked.

"That's a good question," Dulcie mused. "I think she inherited some money initially, or maybe her husband did? They both run an auction house. That's how she became connected with the museum. We bought a small piece from them for the Colonial collection. Had I known it would lead to all this though, I would never have even suggested bidding." Dulcie sipped her beer thoughtfully. "You know, though, now that you mention it, I don't know much about them personally. I should do a little more digging on her."

"Know thy enemy," Dan nodded.

"What's her name?" Nick asked.

Dulcie had just taken a large mouthful of beer. She paused, swallowing. "Vanessa Rich," she replied at last.

Both men laughed.

"Yes, I know. Appropriate, isn't it?" Dulcie added. "I learned it's her married name. I don't know who she was before that. See? Clearly I need to do some research."

"Not like you," Dan said. "You always get the scoop on everyone before you've even met them."

"I know. I'm slacking lately. In my defense though, she did pop onto the scene rather quickly. She joined the board late in the winter and now, suddenly, she's chair. No idea how that transpired."

Nick was thoughtful. "That name sounds familiar. I can't place it though."

Their food arrived and they chatted about other things. After dinner, Dan drifted off in the direction of his boat while Nick walked Dulcie back to her townhouse.

"That name is bugging me," he said, scrunching his hands in the pockets of his worn leather jacket. "I remember an Anderson Rich that I went to law school with. He was about ten years older though, and never spent much time with anyone from the class. But that was down in Boston, so it'd be a pretty big coincidence if it was the same guy's parents up here."

"True," Dulcie said. "But not that much of a stretch." She thought for a moment. "You know, I'm not the sleuth here," she began.

"I beg to differ!" Nick interrupted. Dulcie had been more than instrumental in solving a number of his cases.

"All right, maybe a little," she conceded. "But I just realized that if our *Cruella* here thinks she's going to sell off my office furniture, she'll most likely use her own company."

"I see where you're going," Nick agreed. "But wouldn't she waive her auction house commission if she's the board chair? It would be expected of her, I'd think."

"Oh absolutely. She would have to. But remember, there isn't just a seller's commission but a buyer's commission also. She'd still stand to profit." They had reached Dulcie's doorstep. "Come in for a glass of wine?" she asked, changing the subject.

Nick sighed. "I'd love to, but I have to get up at three-thirty for a stakeout. It's the suspected arson case."

"Ah, yes," Dulcie nodded. "The life of a detective. Not at all what they show in the movies."

"'Fraid not," Nick said. "You get all the glamour," he added.

"Yes, I wish," Dulcie rolled her eyes. She dug for her key in her purse and unlocked the door. "Are you going to kiss me?" she said, turning back toward him.

"Maybe," Nick replied. He pulled her against him and quickly planted a kiss on her lips that lingered for several moments. He lifted her up, set her inside the hallway, then stepped back onto the granite block outside the door. He noticed Dulcie's breath was a bit more rapid than it had been. "Good!" he grinned. "Always have to leave them wanting more! I'll see you tomorrow?"

Dulcie leaned outside the doorway and smacked Nick's arm. "Maybe...!" she replied, mocking him. She heard him laugh as she closed the door.

ॐ

Rupert Hamilton's index finger hovered over the keyboard, waiting to hit the Send button. His lips moved slightly as he reread the email for probably the tenth time. It was certainly unnecessary for him to proofread his own messages so severely, but it had become habit. It wasted some of his time, but at least he was certain of every single word that he committed to the eternity of the digital age.

Words were important to Rupert. Perhaps "word" was not the correct term – more like utterances of communication. His research work focused on bird calls, specifically birds of prey. Every vocalization, every cry, every nuanced squawk was of interest to him. He had observed hundreds of birds personally and poured over thousands of hours of video and recorded calls. It consumed him to the point that he was now dreaming of talking birds.

Rupert knew that he was at the point of obsession but convinced himself that it was temporary. He needed to finish his doctoral thesis and then he would step back, refocus his life, join the *real world* again as his girlfriend so often reminded him.

He glanced down at the keyboard, then back up at the email. "Just send it!" he commanded himself aloud and forced his finger down. The message disappeared, then joined the list of others lined up safely in his Sent box. He knew that they were safe because he backed up everything, every night. Twice.

Rupert sat back in the wooden chair that creaked softly. He heard the noise. He heard the quick chirp of a chickadee outside.

Rupert heard everything.

I made myself into an envelope
into which I could thrust my work deep,
lick the flap, seal it from everybody.
~ Emily Carr

CHAPTER TWO

Shallow puddles had formed on the street, left by the soft rain that had fallen overnight. He dodged them as he crossed, hopping over one deftly. The art museum was just ahead on the other side.

Elias Rich and his wife Vanessa had only moved to Portland recently. He had retired from his job as a financial manager and was looking forward to a new life in a new city.

He was not looking forward to more time with his wife. They had clashed on where exactly to live. Both had agreed on a smaller city, somewhere near the ocean. He had wanted year-round warmth, however. Savannah or perhaps Charleston. She insisted on "the change of seasons" as she put it. As always, her preferences prevailed. Sometimes he believed that she opposed him simply for the sport of it, to establish, and more importantly to win, yet another power play. He sighed, having grown used to it. He'd developed various "sanctuaries" as he liked to call them where he could almost forget about her. Almost.

What irked him, however, was her ability to somehow sense these places and weasel her way in, spoiling them. She was a master at spoiling things. She'd done that with the museum. Shortly after they'd moved to Portland, Elias had begun attending a lecture series at the art museum, something that he thought would never interest her. But before he knew it, she was with him at the lectures, then handing the museum a hefty donation, then on the board of directors, and now elected chair. How that had happened, he had no idea. Well, he had some idea. The money.

It had always been "her" money. Even though he had carefully invested it, nurtured it, built the wealth that they now had, she never let him forget that it began with her. And in Vanessa's mind, it ended with her as well. The auction company was supposed to be a joint venture between them, a sort of retirement job, but of course she was in complete control.

Elias gently opened the outer door of the museum and stepped inside the vestibule. He scuffed off his shoes on the heavy carpet before continuing inside. Passing the information desk, he gave a quick nod and a wave. The attendant didn't need to see his membership card. She knew who he was.

Today he wasn't attending a lecture. He turned toward the worn marble staircase and ascended the steps, two at a time, until he had spiraled his way up through two more floors to the top. His heart was beating harder. Was it from the hasty climb or the anticipation?

In the distance, at the end of the gallery, he could see it. The painting farthest away. His goal. There was nothing overly special about it, it was just the starting point. At last, he reached it and stood, staring intently. Fitz Henry Lane's *Castine Harbor*.

In Elias's mind, the landscapes, or seascapes perhaps in this case, were the best. He found them relaxing. No staring eyes looking back at him. No unspoken requirement for "interpretation" or "understanding" of a jarring abstraction. Just a pretty picture. He felt his heart become steady again and he exhaled slowly.

For the next two hours Elias did what he always referred to in his own mind as "floating." He slowly moved from one work to the next, one room to the next, one floor to the next below, unaware of anyone else. It was a form of meditation. By the time he reached the main floor again, his mind was clear and calm. The raucous voices yelling at him in his brain had all stopped. The difficult memories had been temporarily erased. He could think.

Still standing on the bottom step of the large stone staircase he heard the main door across the gallery open forcefully as a woman blustered in. Elias gripped the handrail hard. He didn't even need to see her – he simply sensed her presence. As stealthily as possible he backed up on the steps until he was out of her sight line. Then he turned and rapidly ran the rest of the way up to the next floor.

Her feet stomped across the marble. Elias heard her exchange a few words that lacked pleasantness with the desk attendant. Then he heard her shoes clacking on the marble again, toward the staircase, closer, then moving beyond. The sound disappeared into the distance. He waited but heard nothing more.

Silently, he descended again. He walked as quickly and quietly as possible across the main gallery floor, skirting the sunbeams that now glowed down from the skylight overhead, and slipped out the door.

Sitting at the reception desk, Rachel had seen him when he had first appeared at the foot of the stairway. She had seen the foreboding, perhaps even fearful expression cross his face. As she spoke with Vanessa Rich, Rachel could see Elias disappearing into the stairwell. Rachel had deliberately spoken with Vanessa more than she normally would have to give Elias a few extra moments. Rachel then busied herself, not looking up, but knowing full well that Elias was making a rapid, one might almost call it terrified, exit.

❈

"Didja find the boat?"

The voice accompanied a paper cup containing steaming coffee that appeared beside Nick's computer. He looked up as his partner, detective Adam Johnson, nestled his large frame down into a battered office chair behind the desk opposite Nick's.

Nick raised the cup in a silent toast, then sipped carefully. "As a matter of fact, the answer is: no." He gestured toward the screen in front of him. "I was just checking weather reports over the past few days, trying to figure out if it drifted somewhere."

"Already did that," Johnson interrupted him.

"Thanks for telling me," Nick replied with a tinge of annoyance.

"But never hurts to check again," Johnson added. He slurped his cup loudly. "OOhh, sorry. Hot!" He put it on the desk in front of him, leaned over, and blew across the top. "So?" he added after several seconds.

"So what?" Nick said.

"So, what was your conclusion?" Johnson said, unperturbed. He resumed blowing steadily across the coffee. His lips, pursed to the point of almost whistling, were surrounded by the stubbles of beard that he'd missed shaving that morning. After years of shaving every day, he'd always thought he'd get better at it. Giving up on shaving wasn't an option for him, though. He thought a gentleman should always have a clean-shaven face. Not that he necessarily qualified as such, but he wanted to look like he was. Besides, his wife liked it.

Nick leaned back in his chair and swiveled it from side to side. "Probably the same as yours," he responded. "A nor'easter came through with gusts over forty miles an hour. The storm system proceeded to just sit there in the gulf for a while before clearing out." He shrugged his shoulders. "My guess is that boat's now floating way offshore by now. If it's still floating."

Johnson nodded in agreement. "Same here. They'll be lucky if they find it off Cape Cod in a month or two at this point."

"Yup," Nick agreed. He reached forward and tapped at his keyboard with one hand, the other still holding the coffee. "And that concludes yet another exciting case in the life of Detective Nicholas Black. Tune in next week...."

Johnson snorted in response. "Hey, don't wish for trouble. We've had our fair share," he added. "I'm staring down retirement and I'd like to just ease out of this place and ease into the next phase of life with as little fanfare as possible."

Nick shook his head. "You know you're as bored as I am," he retorted.

Johnson took another tentative sip from his cup. He nodded without looking up. "Yeah," he said, "You know you're right."

They sat silently while drinking coffee, oblivious to the noises of the police station around them, until a loud voice from the next room drifted in. It was an angry voice.

"Look, I don't care if it isn't actually what *you* would call a murder! She's dead!"

Johnson blinked hard and glanced across at Nick.

Nick's eyes widened as he looked back at his partner. They both stood in unison.

A uniformed officer stuck her head around the corner of the doorway. "Would either of you two gentlemen care to have a chat with this lady who believes that someone murdered her bird?" The officer crossed her eyes at them.

"Why certainly," Johnson replied. "Show her to the interrogation... er, I mean *conference*, room."

"Thank you!" the officer mouthed silently with obvious relief and disappeared again.

Johnson and Nick exchanged glances. Nick swilled down the rest of his coffee while Johnson grabbed a notepad and a pen. He still didn't trust electronic devices entirely. "I can't see electrons," he always said. "I can see paper."

The woman was pacing the room as they entered. She stopped and looked at them intently. Her eyes were close set. '*Like a hawk's*' thought Nick.

"I'm Esmerelda Graves. Who are you?" she demanded.

Johnson introduced himself and extended his hand. She hesitated, then rapidly shook it. '*Fear*' Johnson thought. '*The voice sounds angry, but the hand shows fear.*' As Nick shook the woman's hand, Johnson quickly jotted down the observation. He doubted that Nick had missed it, but wanted to mention it to him later.

"My bird has been murdered," the woman announced after they had all sat down in the somewhat uncomfortable chairs that surrounded the large, fake-woodgrain laminate table. They'd heard that announcement previously but did not convey this to her.

"Go on," Johnson replied calmly.

"I'm a Hawker. A Falconer," the woman explained. "I have several birds that I train. It takes years to properly train one. I went out with my youngest one this morning. We went through the normal routine, but then she didn't respond to my calls. She didn't return."

"Is that unusual?" Nick asked. "Do they always return immediately?"

"No," the woman said simply. "They can get distracted. Especially the new ones. That's why I wasn't overly concerned at first."

"I see," Nick murmured.

"I called and waited, then went to the usual perches, but didn't find her," the woman said.

"How long did this take?" Johnson asked. He had been taking notes as she spoke.

"About half an hour? Perhaps a bit more," the woman replied. "Then I went back to the barn to get the tracking equipment. I put tracking devices on the birds when I take them out, just in case this happens," she explained.

"Good idea," Nick interjected. "Why didn't you have the equipment with you already, though? If this isn't uncommon...."

Esmerelda interrupted him. "You've obviously never seen tracking equipment," she said with annoyance. She held up her hands about two feet apart.

"I've seen it," Johnson interjected smoothly. "Not fun to carry around unless absolutely needed."

"Exactly," Esmerelda replied, glancing at him with a hint of affirmation. She looked back at Nick disapprovingly. "I came back out with the device and found her in the woods. She looked like this," the woman held up her cell phone.

Both men leaned over to see the small screen. On it was what appeared to be a dead bird lying on the ground among scattered leaves and branches.

"Huh!" they both responded at the same time.

"Did you move the body?" Johnson asked. Nick hid his smirk. Johnson was following the questioning pattern of an actual murder. He glanced over at his partner, but Johnson's expression was unreadable.

"Well of course I did!" the woman exclaimed. "I wasn't going to leave her out there! Any animal could have dragged her away and, well...." They all certainly knew the rest.

"Absolutely," Nick replied. He looked at the image again on the phone. "Could you zoom in on that part right there?" he asked, pointing without touching the screen.

"Go ahead yourself," the woman said, sliding the phone closer toward him.

Nick moved the image around with his fingers on the screen, looking more carefully at the bird's legs. "Is this the tracking device?" he asked, pointing to something attached to the bird.

"No, that's for a video recorder," she answered.

"Really?" Both men questioned simultaneously.

"I have a research student working with the birds right now. He's studying the sounds that they make, so he attaches video cameras to them." She gestured again at the screen. Nick noticed scratches on her hand as she did.

Johnson looked up from his notepad. "Would there have been a recording done at the time of the bird's death?" He asked.

Nick still wasn't sure why Johnson seemed to be taking this so seriously but decided to follow his lead. "And how exactly do you know the bird was killed?" he added. "By a person, I'm assuming you mean."

The woman glared at him. "I am *assuming* that because look right here," she moved the phone's image over to another area of the bird. "Her head has a gash on it, as though she was hit by a rock or something hard." She turned to Johnson. "And no, I don't have any video. Rupert only does those when he's working with the birds."

"Who is Rupert?" the men both responded in unison, once again. They glanced at each other. Nick widened his eyes, implying *'cut it out!'* Johnson just shrugged his shoulders.

"Rupert Hamilton. PhD student, working on his dissertation. He's been with the birds for a couple of weeks now," she said.

Nick heard Johnson's pen rapidly scrawling across the page. When he was done, Johnson looked up. "Could we talk to Mr. Hamilton as well?" he asked.

"I would expect you to," the woman bristled.

"Of course," Nick replied smoothly. "One last question. Where is the bird now?"

"In the freezer, where I keep the chicks and mice."

Nick closed his eyes for a moment. *'This just keeps getting weirder and weirder,'* he thought. "The chicks and mice?" he said aloud, opening his eyes again.

"They're dead," the woman added, matter-of-factly. "We use them to train the hawks."

"Ah. Yes. Right then," Nick replied. He wasn't sure if he wanted to know more.

Johnson took down additional notes on how to contact Esmerelda, and they walked her to the front door. "We'll look into this carefully," Johnson said, again shaking her hand. It seemed more steady now.

"Absolutely," Nick added, opening the door for her.

She simply nodded at both of them and left.

Nick turned to Johnson. "What the heck...," he began.

"Wait," his partner replied quickly, holding up his hand as he watched the woman continue down the sidewalk. "Ok, now we can talk. Let's go get a decent coffee," he added. He'd only made it half way through his previous one, the 'office swill' as he referred to it.

They walked down the street toward the local coffee shop, Roasters. It had become their second office. The bell over the door clanged as they went in, and Johnson slid into a nearby booth while Nick got their coffee. It was such a standard routine now that neither questioned it.

Johnson pulled out his notepad as Nick returned to the table. "OK, first question," he said, sliding a cup toward his partner. "Why are you taking this so seriously?"

"I was wondering if you'd noticed," Johnson said.

"Noticed what, that you were taking it seriously?" Nick asked.

"No, noticed *why* I was taking it seriously," he said.

"Apparently not. So again, why are you taking this so seriously?" Nick repeated with slight annoyance.

"Because she was scared," Johnson said simply.

"Scared? You got that from her?" Nick countered.

"Yep. When I shook her hand. She hesitated, then shook it quickly, and her hand was trembling," Johnson explained.

"You sure that wasn't just from anger or frustration?" Nick asked.

"I'm pretty sure. She had that look in her eye, just quickly when she first met us. It was fear. Plus, when she showed you the bird's head on the phone image, her hand was trembling again. She steadied it by putting her arm down on the table to point," Johnson demonstrated with his own arm. "Not a natural way to point at something."

"Yeah, you're right," Nick agreed, looking at Johnson's stubby index finger still pointing as his arm was resting on the table.

"Surprised you didn't pick up on that," Johnson nagged his partner. "Thought I'd trained you better!"

"Uh, that's why we work in teams," Nick retorted. "Two sets of eyes, and all that," he said.

"True enough," Johnson murmured, sipping his coffee. He eased his large bulk backwards along the bench seat until he was sideways, leaning up against the wall. He tipped his head back and looked up toward the ceiling. A fan spun gently overhead creating a soft, cool breeze that Johnson hadn't noticed until now. "Ever go birding?" he asked.

"Like, bird watching?" Nick replied.

"Yeah, or on a bird walk or something? People do that stuff, Johnson said."

"I've been on a bird walk," Nick answered. "It was kind of interesting for the first twenty minutes or so, then I forgot that we were looking for birds and I just hiked along. Not very exciting."

"Um, yeah. Right," Johnson said, his eyes darting away.

"Wait a second! What are you not telling me?" Nick demanded from his partner.

"Nuthin. Just making conversation about birding, that's all," Johnson replied, now gazing out of the large plate-glass window on the opposite side of the room.

"Do you mean to tell me...?" Nick stopped, waiting for Johnson to fill in the blanks.

Johnson swung his legs to the floor and turned back around in his seat to squarely face his partner. He stared Nick down. "Yeah, so I'm a birder. Got a problem with that?"

An image of Johnson loaded down with bird watching gear trying to walk stealthily through rough terrain flashed into Nick's mind. He tried not to grin. "No problem. Nope. None at all. I commend you, in fact. It must take great skill and patience."

"As a matter of fact, it does," Johnson replied defensively. "Not unlike this profession."

"Yes, I see the correlation," Nick said, attempting to remain serious. "So, do you have the equipment? Do you use one of those telescope things and all?"

"Spotting scope," Johnson corrected. "Yes, I do. And before you ask, yes, I keep a life list. I'm just beyond three-hundred different species now, which is not bad."

"Sounds quite formidable if you ask me," Nick said, now unable to hide his grin.

"However, this by no means makes me an expert on our dead hawk," he admitted.

"Murdered hawk," Nick interjected.

Johnson rolled his eyes. "Right. Allegedly. She was a strange one, Ms. Esmerelda Graves. Who has a name like that now, anyway?"

"A strange one," Nick muttered, swigging back the rest of his coffee. "All right, since you're the birder," he grinned again eliciting a scowl from Johnson. "Why don't you go see our new friend and have a look at the bird in the freezer. Meanwhile, I'll go back to the station and run a background check on her. The woman, not the bird. Might be able to get some clues as to whether anyone wants to take down a hawk."

Johnson agreed and slid out from behind the table, a not inconsiderable feat given the size of his stomach. He sighed. His weight loss efforts were a continual struggle. As they left, he eyed the intricate pastry display lovingly but kept walking.

❧

Dulcie strode into her office without looking up and ran headlong into a table. "*OW!*" she exclaimed grabbing her right hip.

Rachel appeared in the doorway. "Look out for that table," she said.

Dulcie glanced over at her with an annoyed look. "Thanks for the warning," she added. "What the heck is this, anyway?" She gestured with one hand, still rubbing her hip with the other.

"That," Rachel said, "is your new desk."

Dulcie eyed it suspiciously then looked back at Rachel. "My what?"

"Yes, you heard that right," Rachel said. "Oh, and here they are," she added. Dulcie could hear a commotion in the hallway outside her door.

"Rachel?" she asked warily. "What is going on?"

Two of the museum's maintenance staff crowded into her office doorway without actually daring to enter entirely. One had a dolly while the other was steering a big, flat cart with wheels. Dulcie had seen these carts before. They were used to move large, heavy objects around the museum. "We're here for the desk, ma'am," one of the two men said.

Dulcie gave Rachel a bewildered look. "Was anyone going to inform me of this?" she asked.

"We just did," Rachel said smoothly. "I only learned about it twenty minutes ago. I was trying to find you," she added.

Dulcie sat on the edge of her desk as if to establish it as her territory. "Do I need the complete story, or is it self-explanatory, given my recent encounter with our new board chair?"

"You know the answer to that," Rachel replied.

Dulcie sighed. She shook her head with resignation. "Give me ten minutes to empty the drawers," she said to the maintenance crew. They both nodded and disappeared leaving the wheeled moving equipment in the hallway.

Rachel walked into the office and shut the door firmly behind her. She knew enough not to say anything just yet.

"She certainly works quickly." Dulcie's words were barely audible.

Rachel had learned that when Dulcie spoke quietly, she was angry. Very, very angry. Rachel had thought to bring a large cardboard box with her, and silently handed it to her boss. "Need help?" was all she dared ask.

Dulcie dumped a large armload of drawer items into the box. Pens, pencils, a stapler, sticky notes...they clattered against each other as she tossed them in. Everything had been organized in the drawers neatly. Now she didn't care.

"What makes her think that she can come marching in here and just take over?" Dulcie asked.

"The fact that the rest of the board elected her chair?" Rachel blurted out unhelpfully.

Dulcie glared at her for a moment, but her stern look quickly softened. "I know, I know. You're right," Dulcie said. "I'm just amazed at how spineless our board actually is," she said. She opened the next drawer with more force than necessary, nearly pulling it completely from the desk. The room was silent for several moments save for the clunking of items against sturdy cardboard.

When she finished, Dulcie hefted the box over to the ugly new table. "What a cheap piece of junk," she exclaimed, shaking her head. She glanced up at Rachel. "Can you get me the current board list, with phone numbers?" she asked. Her voice had grown quiet again.

Rachel quickly nodded and left the room. Dulcie now sat on the table. It sagged slightly under her petite frame, further displaying its lack of quality. She kicked her feet back and forth beneath her. The table bounced up and down. Dulcie didn't notice. She was thinking.

Rachel returned and handed Dulcie the list. "Oh, and there's one more person joining at the next meeting. I don't have their name yet. I'll get it for you, though."

Dulcie scanned the list. "Thanks, Rachel," she said without looking up. "Just trying to figure out how to weather this storm without my head exploding," she added.

"Slight mix of metaphors there I think, but I get the idea," Rachel concluded as she made yet another quick exit.

Dulcie returned to her now empty desk and checked through the drawers one last time. She heard the maintenance crew in the hallway. They peered around the edge of the doorframe.

"Come in," Dulcie announced. "I won't bite. Not you, anyway."

They both laughed nervously and removed the desk as quickly as possible. They repositioned the ugly table so that it now sat where the desk had been, a hideous new focal point to the room. Dulcie stared at it, realizing that she now had nowhere to put any of the items in the cardboard box. She'd need a file cabinet or something similar. She pictured the classic gunmetal gray, slightly dented models that she'd seen by Nick's desk at the police station.

"Seriously, have I become a diva?" she asked the room at large. She knew that she could function just as well without her old desk. It just wasn't the image she thought a museum director should convey.

"Do you want me to answer that question?" a voice from behind her quietly countered.

Dulcie jumped and spun around toward the door. "*Kimberly!*" she exclaimed. The woman laughed as she walked forward and gave Dulcie a quick hug. "It's been ages!" Dulcie added.

Dulcie had met Kimberly Whittimore the year before when she attended a master class given by the museum. The class had not ended well, as the eccentric instructor had died suspiciously halfway through the sessions. Kimberly had been instrumental helping Dulcie, and Nick, bringing the entire episode to a quick conclusion. It had saved both Dulcie's reputation and the museum's. Afterward, Kimberly had hinted at becoming a volunteer docent but had not been able to fully commit, much to Dulcie's disappointment. Dulcie hadn't heard from her for months.

"Yes, ages," Kimberly agreed. "Far too long, and I apologize for that! A few things have happened since I last saw you."

Dulcie hauled a chair over to her new desk-table for Kimberly, then sat down in her own chair. At least Vanessa had allowed her to keep that. For now.

"Nice digs," Kimberly observed, eyeing the laminate surface in front of her and the cardboard box.

Dulcie groaned. "Don't get me started. We have a new board member who managed to weasel herself into becoming chair at lightening speed. She's into cost-cutting, starting with me."

Kimberly shook her head. "Vanessa has no idea who she's up against," she commented.

Dulcie looked surprised. "You know her?"

"I'm about to," Kimberly said slyly. She peered at Dulcie covertly from beneath the silvery bangs of her perfectly cut bob.

"Okay, out with it!" Dulcie ordered.

Kimberly giggled. "Well, let me go back in time a little. The last time I saw you was just after that unfortunate master class, correct?" She didn't wait for Dulcie's answer. "What you don't know is that I took that class because I needed a huge distraction. I'd just retired, you see, and I was looking forward to spending that retirement travelling the world with my husband. Unfortunately, he was looking forward to spending it travelling the world with his secretary."

"Oh, no!" Dulcie exclaimed.

Kimberly put up her hand to stop Dulcie. "No worries, dear," she said. "It all worked out fine once I got over the initial shock. We hadn't been connecting very well for years. I'd thought the travels would help us reconnect, but he simply wanted to disconnect. Ultimately I accepted that and have moved on." Now she looked pointedly at Dulcie. "But not without first securing a very lucrative alimony payment each month! He was a surgeon with a somewhat astronomical salary." Her eyes now glittered mischievously.

Dulcie laughed. "Good for you, then!" she replied. "But what is this with Vanessa? You don't know her yet, but you will?"

"Correct," Kimberly said. She sat forward in her chair, rested her elbows on the table and interlaced her fingers. Cradling her chin in them she said, "You see Dulcie, you're looking at the newest member of the Maine Museum of Art's board of directors!"

The truth of the matter is, the birds
could very well live without us,
but many -- perhaps all -- of us
would find life incomplete,
indeed, almost intolerable
without the birds.
~ Roger Tory Peterson

CHAPTER THREE

"Rupert, darling," the voice drawled. "Fancy a cup of tea?"

Rupert sighed as he looked over at his girlfriend lounging on the couch. She was reading a book. He, on the other hand, was working intently at his computer compiling his latest research notes. She hadn't even glanced at him to see if he was busy. She now turned the page and continued reading.

He would, of course, make the tea. He knew that *she* knew that the mere mention of it would make him want a cup. And she was far more patient. She would simply wait for him to succumb to the desire first, which he always did. Resigned to the inevitable, he reached forward and closed his laptop then padded into the kitchen in stocking feet.

"What kind, Fifi?" he called out. He had learned not to try and guess. It probably wouldn't be correct, and Fiona would simply make not-so-subtle comments such as, "Oh, I do like the Earl Gray better," or something similar.

"That new oolong would be lovely," her voice drifted in. She heard the familiar clattering sounds in the kitchen. Now that he was out of the room she looked up from her book and gazed out the window. The tree branches with their buds just beginning to open waved in the stiff breeze that was pushing the storm system from the night before back out to sea. She couldn't actually see the ocean, of course. They were several miles inland at Esmerelda Graves' farm, living in a small flat above the barn. It certainly wasn't ideal, not as far as Fiona was concerned, but the rent was cheap, and Rupert was happy that he could do his research work so readily.

His bloody research work. It was consuming their lives and Fiona had all she could do to mask her growing annoyance. She'd wanted to get married, settle into a nice cottage perhaps somewhere in Cornwall, and start having children. Rupert kept saying, "When I'm done with my degree, love. I'll be Dr. Rupert Hamilton then and secure a good, solid university position." It had sounded like a wonderful plan in the beginning, but she hadn't counted on his endless and ever-expanding hours of research.

It was the only reason why she had agreed to come to America and live above a barn. He would have full access to whatever he needed with this situation. Plus, Esmerelda had indicated that the lodgings were not "fully winterized" as she put it, meaning that they had to be out by autumn. That suited Fiona just fine. What Rupert needed was a firm deadline.

She heard the kettle whistle and knew he'd be coming back with the tray in a moment. She focused on her book again.

Rupert thunked the tray down gently on the steamer trunk that served as a coffee table. "Fifi, love," he said, pouring her a cup of steaming tea.

"Mmmm?" she replied without looking up.

"Would you like to go over to the art museum tomorrow? Just a little change of scenery? I could say hello to my sister while we're there. I haven't seen her yet since we arrived."

That got Fiona's attention. She put down her book, slid her legs off the couch, and placed her feet on the floor. She took the cup that he held out to her. "I would love to, on one condition."

"Anything, dear," he replied.

She tried not to look at him with disdain. The 'anything, dears' never seemed to quite materialize. She masked her annoyance by taking a sip of tea. Regaining composure, she said, "I'd also like for you to take me to dinner. Nothing fancy, mind you. I know we don't have much to spare here. But just a change of pace."

"That sounds perfect," Rupert replied. He filled his own cup, from the little teapot they'd brought from

England, added a dollop of milk, then went back to his laptop.

Fiona stared at the back of his head for a few moments. She'd seen entirely too much of it lately. Then she sighed, swung her legs back up on the couch again, adjusted the pillows slightly, and reopened her book.

❧

Vanessa Rich scanned the list of board members, stopping when her eyes reached the last one. She was new – Kimberly Whittimore. Vanessa had done her research on all the others but didn't know a thing about this new one. She had to hurry and dig up a few choice items before the next meeting.

Vanessa managed to locate the dirt on everyone. She was amazingly adept at it. It was her leverage, her strength, her source of power. If anyone was giving her a difficult time, she'd simply make an allusion to whatever it was that was unsavory in that person's past. She never had to say much. 'Polite company' was called just that for a reason – they always kept conversation to a polite level, never daring to descend to unpleasantness, even if it meant not defending themselves. Once she hinted at a confrontation, an embarrassment, they were far more apt to let her have her way and then quickly change the subject.

She turned to her computer and typed in Kimberly's name. "Hmmmmm," she muttered aloud. Career as a nurse, mostly, it appeared. Recently divorced. That could be interesting. She typed in the name of

Kimberly's former husband. Vanessa's eyes lit up and a twisted smile spread across her face. So, he was a surgeon! Money there, for sure. That explained how Kimberly made that big donation to get on the board. And the ex probably dumped Kimberly for a younger model with a tad less mileage on her. Vanessa made a mental note to ask the more gossipy board members about details. Subtly, of course.

ભ

Adam Johnson pulled up to the old barn that was now a falconry center. He looked up at it carefully while still sitting in the car. Locations could tell a story, and that was important. Any detail could break a case open.

He chuckled to himself, realizing that he was taking this 'murdered bird' issue as seriously as any other case. That was a good thing, though. He reminded himself that if it had been a horse, a cow, a dog... the humane society would surely have become involved. He was surprised that they weren't already. Maybe this was different somehow?

The driveway and the grounds surrounding the barn were meticulously kept. The barn itself looked as though it was in very good repair, so much so that it was difficult for him to tell how old it was. He glanced up and saw windows in the upper floor, then noticed a skylight on one section of the roof. '*Offices upstairs, maybe?*' he thought. At that moment he saw a shadow walk in front of the center window, stop, as if to peer down, then disappear.

Johnson got out of his car, and within seconds Rupert Hamilton slid open the heavy, oversized door. He stepped outside and waited for Johnson to reach him.

"Hello," Rupert said. "Are you here to see the birds or Esmerelda?"

"Both, if possible," Johnson replied.

"Well I'm afraid you'll only be half-way successful. Esmerelda is out on an errand, so it's just me right now. I'm Rupert Hamilton. Can I help you with something?"

Johnson scratched his head. Rupert seemed very forthcoming. Johnson decided to come straight to the point. He stuck out his hand and shook Rupert's. "I'm detective Adam Johnson. Earlier Ms. Graves came to the police station to report a dead bird. 'Murdered' she said. Can you tell me anything about that?"

A cloud seemed to cross Rupert's face. "Ah, yes. Igraine, the newest of the bunch. Esmerelda was quite upset. She said it looked as though someone had thrown a rock at her. Hit her directly on the head. They must have had good aim. She either died from that or when she hit the ground. Want to see?"

Rupert's manner was very matter-of-fact. Johnson had already pulled out his notebook and was taking notes. He made another about Rupert's demeanor. "Can I ask what your position is here?" Johnson said, dropping the hand with the pencil to his side. He knew from years of questioning that people were more apt to talk, less intimidated, if you hid the pencil as much as possible. Watching someone write down everything that they said was nerve wracking.

"I'm doing research on the birds," Rupert replied. "I'm getting my doctorate in linguistics."

Johnson's brow wrinkled. "Linguistics?" he said.

Rupert laughed and quickly added, "Yes, I know. Doesn't make sense immediately. I'm studying bird calls and sounds, specifically the hawks here. I'm correlating them to their actions and interactions with each other. I've outfitted some of them with tiny video cameras so I can keep track of how they sound when they do various things." He took a quick breath. "You see, there's a theory that the earliest human languages, not even a written language but older than that, could be partially based on bird songs. The ancient Hindu chant the Rigveda has been passed down orally and is perhaps three to four-thousand years old. Some scholars who've studied it have found similarities to bird songs. I'm trying to continue that work, looking at various species of birds." He spoke quickly, with increasing excitement, and now paused again to breathe.

It was obvious that Rupert was consumed by his work. Johnson knew the type, realizing that he had to keep Rupert on track, or he would talk about his research endlessly. "Could you show me the bird? Igraine, you called her?" Johnson interjected before Rupert could continue.

"Sure," he answered. "Follow me."

They entered the dimly lit barn and walked through toward the back. As Johnson's eyes adjusted to the low light, he could see large caged off areas. Each contained a bird on a roost. Some squawked loudly as the two men went by.

"Easy, Arthur!" Rupert called out to one of them. "That's King Arthur," he said over his shoulder. "He likes to *think* he's the king, anyway." Johnson wondered if there was literally a pecking order, but didn't want to introduce a tangent for Rupert to follow in the conversation.

They reached the back of the barn where Rupert led Johnson into what appeared to be an office space. He squinted in the glare as Rupert flipped on the light. Once again waiting for his eyes to adjust, he looked around the room. A tall table in the corner beneath a small window contained a scale. On a whiteboard behind it Johnson could see a list of names, each with a corresponding weight.

Rupert was already at the back of the room where he pried up the the lid of a large freezer. He carefully lifted out a plastic bag that seemed to be filled with feathers. Carrying it to the table, he put it down, opened it, and pulled out the lifeless body that was once Igraine.

"Here's the gash," he said, moving the bird's head around as best he could, given that it was now entirely frozen. Johnson noticed the care that Rupert seemed to take, holding the bird gently, almost as though she were still alive.

"May I?" asked Johnson, reaching his hand out toward the bird. Rupert gave him what seemed to be a reluctant look, but put Igraine back down on top of the plastic bag and stepped aside. Johnson lifted her carefully, looking at the body, tail, wings, and finally the head. "That is odd," he concluded, putting the bird back down on the plastic bag. "Not even the wings seemed to be damaged other than ruffled feathers. Just the head."

"Yeah, that's exactly why Esmerelda thinks someone killed her," Rupert said.

Johnson nodded. "And, if I had to guess, I'd say it wasn't a fall that did it. Neither the wings nor the tail look damaged so I doubt she fell very far. Do you know if she was beneath any tall trees?"

"No. She wasn't." The loud voice behind them made both men jump. Johnson turned quickly. He didn't like being caught off guard.

"In fact," Esmerelda said, waving them both aside as she approached the table, "I can take you to the exact spot where I found her." She gazed at Igraine's lifeless body for several moments, ignoring the two men, then put the bird back in the plastic bag. She returned it to the freezer.

'*That's odd*,' thought Johnson. Esmerelda didn't seem to show any affection toward the bird. Perhaps she didn't view them as pets? They were part of her business and what appeared to be her life's work. Maybe she had learned not to become emotionally attached for that reason? It was probably not unlike a farmer raising animals to sell, or worse, he reasoned with himself.

Esmerelda shut the freezer lid decisively and turned back toward them. "This way," she said and marched out the door.

Johnson immediately followed as instructed before realizing that he'd never actually agreed to hike out to the scene of the crime. Then again, it was quite literally 'the scene of the crime' so it was expected that he would go. He shook his head. This was really getting strange.

Rupert stayed back in the barn as Esmerelda and Johnson left and headed into the woods. They followed a vague trail through the low-lying bushes. Their springtime flowers were just beginning to emerge. Johnson noticed how Esmerelda walked quickly but almost silently through the undergrowth.

As if reading his mind, she said over her shoulder, "You're a quiet walker. Unusual for a man, especially of your size."

Johnson snorted at the blunt comment. He could have taken it as rude, but he was beginning to understand Esmerelda. She was one of those rare people who didn't register emotion – in herself or anyone else. She took everything, and everyone, at face value, and probably expected them to do the same. Or didn't care.

"Not my first bird walk," Johnson replied. At that moment a cardinal swooped in front of them. "Still seems strange to see cardinals in Maine. They were never here when I was a kid."

That got Esmerelda's attention. She stopped short and wheeled around. Johnson nearly plowed into her and had to take a quick step backwards. "You know your birds," she stated with a hint of surprise. "Good." She turned back around and continued walking.

Johnson grinned for a moment as he followed her. He liked catching people off guard. They revealed a lot more that way.

They came to a clearing and Esmerelda walked toward the center. She pointed to the ground. "Right here," she said.

Johnson joined her, knelt down with a soft grunt and examined the ground where she pointed. Nothing seemed amiss. He looked up. No trees were directly above them. He stood and slowly walked in a circle around the spot, scanning the ground back and forth.

"What are you doing?" Esmerelda asked.

"I'm looking to see if there's any obvious object that could have been used as a weapon. A rock that seems out of place or something like that."

Esmerelda raised her eyebrows but said nothing.

"Yes, it's a bit of a longshot, but it's worth doing just to rule it out. Quick and easy, plus it gives me a better sense of the scene," he said. He didn't feel any need to justify his actions, but thought she'd appreciate an explanation.

She did. "That makes sense," she acknowledged. She liked it when things made sense. Things were supposed to make sense. That's why she worked with birds rather than people. Birds made sense. People didn't.

Johnson stopped walking in circles and pulled out his cell phone. Nick had taught him how to take pictures with it. He had complained about it at the time, but secretly was beginning to see all of the ways it came in handy. He zoomed in with several shots of the area where the bird had been found, then backed up and took several more of the entire clearing. Finally, he did one last panorama shot of the entire clearing showing as much of the surrounding trees as he could.

"Okay, I think that's all I can do here for now," he said to Esmerelda. She nodded and silently led him back to the barn. Johnson could hear one of the birds squawking inside. He reached into his pocket and fished out his card. "One last thing," he said. "Could you send me the photos that you took when you found Igraine?" He pointed to his email address on the card.

"Right," Esmerelda said. A loud, long screech emerged from the barn. "Arthur's in need of some attention," Esmerelda said, unmoved. "I'll see to him, then send you the pictures."

"Perfect," Johnson said, extending his hand. She shook it dismissively, then went into the barn, disappearing in the comparative darkness.

Johnson stared into the gaping hole of a doorway for a few moments, trying to take everything in. Something wasn't quite adding up, but he couldn't put his finger on what was niggling at him. He went back to his car.

As he slowly navigated around a large pothole in the long driveway, he looked in his rearview mirror. He could clearly see Rupert in the upstairs window. Esmerelda had reemerged outside, now carrying what Johnson assumed to be the bird Arthur on her gloved hand. Rupert was watching the bird intently.

◌੪

Nick sat at his desk in the midst of the police station communal office space and rubbed his eyes. He'd been looking at the computer screen for nearly two hours and his head ached. The background check that he'd done on Esmerelda Graves seemed clean enough. A few parking tickets. One speeding ticket. He'd learned that she'd spent time in the Caribbean as well. His brain now pictured her in a sarong and sunglasses holding a fruity rum drink, and he instantly regretted it. Esmerelda Graves was not even close to the sarong and sunglasses type.

The Virgin Islands. She'd been down there for a little over a year, two years prior, then had returned occasionally. She had a local bank account, but then that wasn't surprising given she'd lived there. And unlike most Caribbean islands, St. John was part of the United States, not technically "offshore" so she couldn't have hidden money away. Or not easily, at any rate.

She owned the property where she currently lived, in the quiet town of Cumberland, just beyond Portland. No mortgage. She'd bought it with cash around the time that she returned from the year-long stint on St. John. Before that she appeared to have lived in various places, fliting around like a bird.

Like a bird. Was the Caribbean sojourn all about birding? That seemed to be her life. Judging by her reaction to the dead hawk, it was the focal point of her life. '*Murdered hawk,*' he reminded himself.

Who would report a murdered bird? Nick tried to think about it in a different way. If someone found their dog shot, would they be upset enough to report it to the police, claiming it was murdered? They probably would. It was a strange thing to do – kill someone else's pet. He could only think of three reasons why someone would do something like that: anger, fear, or revenge. Which one was it?

Perhaps he was getting ahead of himself. He hadn't heard back from Johnson. He might have decided that the bird wasn't killed by someone. Intentionally, anyway. In that case it would just be manslaughter. Or birdslaughter.

Nick sighed and pushed his chair back from the desk. As he stood, Johnson came into the room. "Ah, just the man I'm looking for," Johnson said. "Care to take a walk?"

"I would absolutely love to take a walk," Nick replied, logging out of his computer. "I'm not exactly turning up pay dirt here. How'd you make out?"

Johnson didn't reply immediately. He waited until they were outside and well down the street. It was a common habit for both of them – to start a conversation, pause at length, then continue. Anyone following and attempting to listen wouldn't be able to hear everything without making themselves obvious. At last Johnson continued. "Very odd woman, but we knew that."

"Yep," Nick agreed.

"She wasn't there at first. A guy named Rupert Hamilton showed me the bird, who's name was Igraine, by the way."

Nick looked at Johnson quizzically, but he didn't elaborate on the name. "Seems Rupert is a doctoral candidate working with the birds to research their calls. Something about linguistics and ancient human language. Anyway, he showed me the now frozen

Igraine who was most certainly smacked on the head from behind with something. No other injuries anywhere that I could see. No bite marks to show another animal had carried her along then dropped her on the ground. Intact wings, tail... just some ruffled feathers."

Nick chuckled at the metaphor.

"Yeah, I know," Johnson continued. "But speaking of that, Esmerelda came in just as we were done with the bird. She took me out to the 'scene of the crime', if you will."

Again, Nick chuckled.

Johnson ignored him this time. "I'd been mostly skeptical about her whole complaint until then. I mean, it could have been an accident even though the injury did seem strange. But the scene makes me think otherwise. It was a clearing in the woods, an open area, with no large trees directly around. Our bird couldn't have fallen and smacked her head that way. There weren't any markings on the ground to indicate a fight or a scuffle. No feathers caught in low bushes or anything. The scenario I see is that she was flying over the clearing, someone threw an object at her, it smacked her on the head, and she dropped to the ground. Oh, and she couldn't have been flying very high because if she had, she'd probably have injured something else, like a wing or her tail, when she hit the ground."

"Okay, but what about this," Nick interjected. "What if someone was carrying her, smacked her on the head, then just dumped her on the ground in the woods?" he asked.

They both paused, waiting for the stop light to change so they could cross the street. They walked for another block before Johnson continued. "Thought about that," he said. "Why would someone do that? Wouldn't they try to bury the body? Or at least break a wing or something to make it look like an accident?"

"Unless they didn't want it to look like an accident," Nick replied.

"Like a warning?" Johnson mused. "No, I don't' think so. If that was the case, I think it would have been more obvious. But I did get the feeling that Esmerelda was still afraid of something. Maybe afraid isn't quite the right word. Worried? Concerned?"

"If you found a pet killed, wouldn't you be worried and concerned?" Nick countered. He didn't expect an answer. They'd reached the waterfront now and continued out onto one of the docks. Nick stopped and leaned against a tall piling, watching a fishing boat navigate its way into the harbor. Johnson stopped as well, shoved his hands into his pockets, and looked down into the water below. A school of tiny little fish were swarmed around the barnacles that encrusted the piling under the water.

"Background?" Johnson prompted his partner.

"Not much although there's a stint in the Caribbean," Nick replied.

Johnson's eyebrows went up.

"Yeah, I know," Nick agreed. "The Virgin Islands. St. John, to be specific, so still in the country technically. She was there a couple years back for over a year, then has made a trip back for about a month each year since.

Could be nothing, even if it is the Caribbean. Plenty of people go there for less than nefarious reasons."

"What about money?" Johnson asked.

"No signs of anything major although she did buy the place in Cumberland with cash," Nick said. "Still, for a lot of people three-hundred grand isn't necessarily a huge amount to have readily available. She had no sources of overly large income that I could see. No police record other than traffic tickets. Seems she does mostly hawk training for work. Is that lucrative?"

"Maybe she had a good client on St. John?" suggested Johnson.

"Good point," said Nick. "That's entirely possible. It'd explain going back there as well."

"Yup," Johnson agreed. He'd seen Nick watching the fishing boat and now followed its progress too. It was getting closer. A deck hand had emerged and began hauling barrels to one side. The man reminded him of Rupert – same build and hair color. "Something seemed odd about the guy there with Esmerelda," Johnson said.

Nick turned and looked at his partner. "Odd?"

"Yeah. I mean, I think he's legit. Seems to know his stuff and obviously cares about the birds." He remembered how gently Rupert had held Igraine even though she was dead. "Just got a strange feeling about him. Can't quite figure it out."

"Think I should run a check on him as well?" Nick asked.

"Wouldn't hurt," Johnson said.

They both looked out across the horizon. The sun was high in the sky now, and a warm spring breeze drifted over them. Neither wanted to move just yet.

Finally, Nick pushed himself away from the wooden piling and turned back toward the city. Johnson followed. As they continued back up the dock, Johnson mused, "Bet you never thought you'd be solving the case of a murdered bird. Kind of Agatha Christie, don't you think?"

Nick smiled. "Very much, although she'd follow it up with a dead person."

"Don't even say that," Johnson admonished. "I'll take a bird over a person any day of the week."

Me too," Nick agreed. "Me too."

When the bird and the book disagree,
believe the bird.
~ John James Audubon

CHAPTER FOUR

"Rupert!"

Rachel's exclamation filtered through the closed door of Dulcie's office. She walked over, opened it, and poked her head around the corner.

"I'm so glad to see you!" Dulcie heard Rachel nearly squeal.

Now Dulcie had to find out who this was. She'd never heard Rachel mention a 'Rupert' before. Was he an old boyfriend? A long-lost cousin? Dulcie walked out to the main gallery to see Rachel hugging a man who bore striking similarities to her. Rachel glanced over and caught sight of Dulcie on the other side of the room. "Dulcie, come meet my brother!" she announced.

Dulcie, with eyes widening, looked quickly at Rachel. "How did I not know that you have a brother?" Dulcie asked as she joined them.

"What?" Rupert said with mock indignation. "Rachel, how could she not know...."

"Oh, shut up!" Rachel retorted, laughing.

"Dulcie, this is my half-brother," she emphasized the 'half', "Who hides himself away somewhere in England."

"That's true enough," Rupert said. He extended his hand and shook Dulcie's. "Rupert Hamilton, at your service madam," he added.

"Well, again, I will ask, how could I not know you have a half-brother?" Dulcie repeated.

"Because we ...," Rupert and Rachel both spoke at once. Rachel made a face at Rupert then continued. "We haven't seen each other in about three years now, I think. Is that right, Rupert?"

"A little over three," Rupert replied.

Rachel turned to Dulcie. "I guess he never came up in conversation. Which is ironic since Rupert is a linguist. But he prefers being an obscure linguist, I think. He's usually in the dark and dreary corners of a university building, so his life is less than compelling."

"Hey!" Rupert exclaimed. Rachel elbowed him.

Dulcie nodded. "Starting to make more sense," she said.

"We have the same father," Rachel added. "Rupert grew up in the UK with our dad. I grew up here with my mom and my step-father."

"Which explains the resemblance," Dulcie said.

"Appearance, yes. Personality, no," Rupert replied. "Rachel is the ever-efficient businesswoman. I'm the inefficient scholar."

"Well said!" Rachel interjected.

"What brings you here?" Dulcie asked Rupert.

"My research, of course. The guiding force of my life," he replied. "I'm working with birds right now. Hawks. I'm studying their calls and comparing them to early human language."

Dulcie's surprised look was obvious. "That sounds very ambitious and really interesting! How did you...," Dulcie stopped mid-sentence as she caught sight of a shadow looming in the foyer of the museum. She groaned. "Rachel, it's Cruella," she said in a hushed voice.

Rachel groaned as well under her breath. "Board of trustees chair Vanessa Rich," she whispered to her brother. "We call her Cruella de Vil."

Rupert croaked a soft sound of congenial dismay in response.

The overbearing woman opened the inner glass door forcefully and looked across the room. She caught sight of Dulcie. Jerking her head in the direction of Dulcie's office, she marched out of the main gallery, obviously intending that Dulcie should follow.

Dulcie sighed heavily. "What did I do to deserve this?" she stated to the room at large. Turning back to Rachel and her brother, she said, "I'd love to talk more at some point. Let's have lunch or dinner or something."

"I'd love to," Rupert said.

"Good! We'll have Rachel organize it. She's very efficient!" Dulcie winked at them, then sighed again as she walked across the large gallery toward her office.

Rachel turned back to her brother. She'd just remembered that he'd mentioned bringing his girlfriend with him on his extended trip. "Where's Fiona?" she asked. "I'm dying to meet her!"

"And so you shall," Rupert replied. "She woke up with a sore throat, so she wanted to stay home and rest. I left her with a large pot of chicken soup."

"As any good boyfriend would," Rachel said.

"Absolutely," Rupert agreed. "I'm sure she'll be better in a day or two. Let's figure out when we can all get together."

Rachel led him over to the main desk in the front hall and began looking at the museum schedule on the computer. They chatted as they did and eventually settled on a day. Rupert scribbled it down on a slip of paper, waved to his sister, and left.

Rachel waited until the gallery was relatively silent again, then crept over to Dulcie's door. She could just barely make out the conversation. It did not sound friendly.

Inside her office, Dulcie was trying to remain calm. She sat behind the hideous table with most of the items that had been in her old desk drawers now still in the cardboard box on the floor. Vanessa was eyeing the armoire in the corner.

"Mahogany, I'd venture to guess," she said.

Dulcie couldn't stand it any longer. "And where shall I hang my coat if that's gone, too?" she heard herself blurt out. Her regret was instantaneous.

Vanessa turned slowly. Her squinted eyes raked over Dulcie. "Perhaps on the back of your chair, like everyone else," she said quietly. "Tell that assistant of yours to have maintenance come get this as soon as possible," she continued.

Dulcie said nothing. There was nothing to say. Actually, there was a great deal to say but nothing that would help Dulcie in the current situation, so she held her tongue with difficulty.

Vanessa looked over at the door. She could have sworn she heard someone outside.

Fortunately for Rachel, Vanessa was a stomper. At the last moment Rachel heard Vanessa stomp across the room. Rachel darted into the main hall again. Vanessa wrenched open the door quickly, looking back and forth. She didn't see anyone.

'Is this woman a paranoid lunatic on top of everything else?' thought Dulcie. She made a mental note to ask Nick what the specific traits of a paranoid lunatic were. If anyone would know, he would.

"Hmmmm," Vanessa muttered. "All right," she said, stepping back into the office. "Oh, yes. One more question. Who is this new board member?"

"Her name is Kimberly Whittimore," Dulcie said curtly.

"Yes, I know that much," Vanessa barked. "Who is she?"

Dulcie quickly decided that she would not reveal the fact that she and Kimberly already knew each other. Something told her to keep that bit of information to herself. "She's lived in the area for quite a while," Dulcie said. "She's retired now, I believe. She made a sizable donation to the museum."

"Where'd her money come from?" Vanessa asked bluntly.

'The term crass does not begin to describe this woman,' Dulcie thought as she eyed Vanessa cautiously. "I really don't know," Dulcie said aloud. "You'll have to ask her," she added innocently.

Vanessa gave Dulcie a withering look. "I'll ask some of the other board members," she replied haughtily. "Oh, and I assume you'll be attending our next meeting?" she added.

Dulcie stood and walked toward the door. It was a subtle attempt to get Vanessa out of her office. Fortunately, this time it actually appeared to work. "Of course," she said, holding the door open widely. "I wouldn't miss it for the world."

Vanessa glared at her one last time, then left.

ଔ

"Oh, bloody hell!" Rupert said as he clapped his hands together.

Fiona jumped, startled by his sudden outburst. "What's wrong?" she croaked. Her sore throat had become steadily worse throughout the day.

"Sorry, Fifi. Didn't mean to frighten you. I just remembered something."

"Was it important?" Fiona asked, lying back on the couch. She adjusted the warm woolen blanket around her again.

"Yes, and I can't believe I forgot. I have to retrieve the camera from Arthur."

"Did you go out with him today?" Fiona asked. She waved her hand vaguely toward the window.

"Yes, early this morning. You were still asleep. I didn't want to wake you," he said.

"That was very kind," Fiona replied feebly. Her voice was now more like a cackle. She closed her eyes.

"Yes, but now I'm not being quite so thoughtful. Sorry to bother. You rest now, okay? I'll be quiet, I promise," he added.

"Mmmmm," Fiona mumbled in response.

Rupert gave her a pat on the shoulder then quietly left her on the couch to nap. He needed to retrieve the camera and was annoyed with himself that he'd forgotten. He quietly made his way downstairs, avoiding the fourth step with its annoying squeak.

As Rupert neared King Arthur's aviary the bird spread his wings half way, rumpling his fathers against his back. He called out softly.

"Shhhh! Easy," Rupert replied. He opened the cage door and went in. Arthur was on the top part of his perch, as usual. He liked to be up high most of the time, Rupert had discovered. He slowly approached being careful not to make actual eye contact. Arthur seemed to perceive that as a threat, or perhaps a challenge. Rupert was still trying to determine which.

Rupert glided his hand over to Arthur's leg. The camera was latched to a plastic band that stayed attached to Arthur. Rupert pressed a small button on the band and the camera detached. He slipped it into his closed fist as he moved his hand away.

Suddenly, Arthur turned his head sharply. His yellow eyes glared directly at Rupert, then he slammed his beak down onto Rupert's hand.

"Ooowww!" Rupert heard himself wail as he instinctively jumped away. Arthur now looked over at Rupert calmly as though nothing had happened.

"You little bastard!" Rupert exclaimed. His hand was bleeding and hurt badly from the force of Arthur's strong, sharp beak. "No wonder you can kill those rodents so easily!" Rupert said. He then remembered the camera and was glad he'd closed his fist around it. He darted through the aviary door, closed it behind him, and went into the office. Flicking on the light he went over to the sink, dropped the camera onto the counter beside it, and immediately began running cold water over his hand. "Dammit," he swore. The cut was deep. He should probably see a doctor. He might even need a stich or two.

Turning off the water, he grabbed a wad of paper towels and held them hard against the cut. He thought about what to do next. The bleeding didn't seem to be slowing down.

Rupert rummaged through a drawer and found some first-aid ointment. He took off the paper towels and applied the ointment as best he could, then pulled off a fresh wad of towels and pressed them back on the wound. "Well, I certainly can't drive like this," he muttered. Fiona wouldn't be able to drive him either, not after the large dose of cold medicine she'd just taken.

He heard someone out in the barn. Looking through the door, he saw Esmerelda. "Can you help?" he called out to her. Hearing the concern in his voice, she rushed in.

"What happened?" she exclaimed looking at the now scarlet paper towels pressed against his hand.

"Arthur," Rupert said. "I went in to get the camera just like I have before. Everything seemed normal, but then, out of the blue, he snapped his beak into me! Just the once, too. Really odd."

"That is odd," said Esmerelda. She was staring at the bloody paper towels. Her eyes moved over to the wad that Rupert had put down previously. She reached behind him, grabbed them from the counter, and threw them in the trash.

Turning back to Rupert she said, "All right, let me see."

"It's pretty bad," Rupert said, still holding the paper towels over the wound.

Esmerelda looked up at him. "I watch birds of prey devour rodents every day. That isn't pretty. I think I can handle this."

Rupert nodded and removed the toweling. Esmerelda took one quick look, then said, "You're right. Get in the car. Is Fiona upstairs?"

"Yes, but she's asleep probably. She's sick."

"I'll drive you then. I'll leave a note for her."

Rupert got in the car. When Esmerelda joined him, she said, "There's an urgent care medical center in the next town. Under ten minutes. Will that work?"

Rupert nodded. He wished he brought the entire roll of paper towels with him. His other hand was now stained with blood as it soaked through the thick paper. When they reached the medical center, Esmerelda pulled up to the door. "You go in, I'll park and meet you."

Rupert didn't even reply. He quickly lurched out of the car and inside. He was beginning to feel dizzy.

A nurse took one look at him as he came through the door and immediately sat him in a wheelchair. She steered him into another room where Rupert watched her remove the paper towels. Everything was beginning to swim around him.

"What's your name?" he heard someone calling from the distance. "Sir? Your name?" Rupert wondered why they were so far away and speaking so quietly.

He woke up on a gurney ten minutes later. His hand was bandaged and throbbing. His blurry eyes finally focused, and he realized Esmerelda was standing beside him, talking to the nurse. "I'm back," Rupert said.

The nursed turned and chuckled. "Well, we're glad of that!" she said.

"I passed out, obviously," Rupert said. "Was it loss of blood?"

The nurse tilted her head sideways. "You might say that," she replied. "You really didn't lose enough to make you pass out, though," she began.

"Really?" Rupert exclaimed. "Because seriously, it looked like rather a lot of it!"

"Nope," the nurse said. "It was the sight of it. Some people are fine with a little, but then it just gets overwhelming. Especially when it's their own."

"And now I feel like an idiot," Rupert interjected.

"Don't," the nurse replied. "I've seen it happen more often than not. It's pretty common, really." She turned to Esmerelda. "What's your relationship with our patient here?"

"Colleague," Esmerelda stated simply.

"Can I give you instructions for medication?" the nurse asked.

"I don't think my brain has been affected," Rupert said.

"All right then, I'll just tell both of you," the nurse continued. "Antibiotics, of course. Change the dressing each morning and evening until it stops oozing. And you have two stiches. Come back in ten days and we'll see how you're doing with those. We'll remove them as soon as we can."

Rupert nodded.

"I have to say," the nurse added. "I've never seen an injury like that. I had no idea a bird could peck that hard. I knew their beaks were strong, but that was a deep wound!"

"You'd be surprised," Esmerelda said. "I've seen one take down a rabbit larger than himself."

The nurse shuddered. "Nature is brutal sometimes, I guess."

"Every creature has to eat," Esmerelda said coldly.

The nurse stared at her for a moment, then shifted her gaze to Rupert. "All right then. You're all set, Rupert. Get some rest and take care of yourself." She tapped the instruction sheet that she had given him.

Rupert nodded. "Can I get off this contraption now?" he asked, looking down at the gurney.

"Slowly," she said. "And only if you feel steady."

Rupert put his arms down to each side of him to support his weight as he hoisted himself off but winced as his bandaged hand made contact. He shifted his weight to his good hand, leaned forward and slid down to a standing position. He felt a little light-headed but wasn't going to admit it.

"Excellent. Well, then," the nurse said. "I'll walk you out."

The cooler air outdoors felt good on Rupert's face. He inhaled deeply and slowly as he followed Esmerelda, willing himself to put one foot in front of the other. They reached the car, and he got in.

Esmerelda slid behind the wheel. As she pulled out of the parking lot she said, "Very odd how Arthur reacted. They always have a reason for doing whatever they do. I'd like to know why."

"Me too," Rupert said. He leaned his head against the back of the seat and closed his eyes. He felt slightly nauseous and cracked open the window. Esmerelda drove them back to the barn and helped him in.

Fiona jumped up as they clomped up the stairs of the apartment. She took one look at Rupert and said, "What on Earth is going on?" Rupert noticed that her voice was still a thin, croaking sound.

"Got in a tussle with a hawk," Rupert said. "I lost round one."

"Well I hope there won't be any round two!" Fiona exclaimed.

"Did I wake you?" he asked. He turned to Esmerelda. "Fiona's sick," he said simply.

Esmerelda rolled her eyes. "Yes, you mentioned that before. Aren't you the pair. I'll leave you to it. Looks like you'll likely be all right, just uncomfortable at most." She looked over at Fiona as she stuffed a wad of tissues onto her nose to cover an enormous sneeze. "Same goes for you," Esmerelda said.

Rupert thanked Esmerelda as she clomped back down the stairs. He saw Fiona wince as Esmerelda hit the fourth step, making it squeal. Fiona hated that sound.

"I think we'd both best get something into us, then go to bed," Rupert said.

Fiona nodded. She stumbled to the refrigerator, pulled out two containers of yogurt and handed one to Rupert. He tried to open it but couldn't with only one functioning hand. Fiona sighed, reached over, and pulled the cover off. "Yes, aren't we the pair," she rasped hoarsely. They would have laughed, but it really wasn't funny.

I am not strong on perfection.
~ Jasper Johns

CHAPTER FIVE

"Report from the treasurer?" Vanessa Rich's voice snapped out the phrase as though it was an order rather than a request. That's because it was.

The board members of the Maine Museum of Art, sitting around the long and highly polished walnut table, shifted uncomfortably in their seats. Dulcie heard a few chairs scrape against the floor as their occupants instinctively slid ever so slightly away from Vanessa. '*Preparation for escape if the viper should attack,*' thought Dulcie. She noticed her heart rate increasing. This was not good.

The treasurer, a small man with a shining dome of a head, cleared his throat gently. He handed out sheets of paper with columns of numbers to everyone around the table, then cleared his throat again. "As you can see, the past month has brought in some new revenue, so we've been able to pay down the...,"

"Oh, hush!" Vanessa interjected.

The man stopped talking and adjusted his glasses without looking up at her.

"Yes, the sale of the desk brought down some of the debt. That's good." Vanessa continued to scan the report. The room was silent as each person stared down at the long list in front of them.

Dulcie glanced up at Kimberly across the table from her. Kimberly looked back at her, over at Vanessa, then back at Dulcie. She winked.

'*Oh no,*' Dulcie thought. '*Kimberly's going to say something!*' Dulcie realized she was holding her breath.

"Vanessa," Kimberly said. "I'm new here, obviously. Could you please explain what you just said? A desk was sold?" She looked at Vanessa innocently.

Dulcie heard the simultaneous sharp intake of breath from the people sitting on either side of her. Vanessa was not to be questioned. They knew they were about to witness a full assault.

Vanessa's eyes narrowed. She gave Kimberly a very long, hard stare. Usually this was enough to silence anyone that dared to address Vanessa directly.

Kimberly continued to gaze at Vanessa innocently.

"I believe you haven't been formally introduced," Vanessa said, changing the subject. "This is our new board member, Kimberly Whittimore," she announced without taking her eyes off Kimberly. "She's recently provided a sizeable donation, for which we thank her.

And we should of course thank her ex-husband as well," Vanessa smiled slyly. She had emphasized the "ex" part.

Kimberly was not so easily defeated. She laughed and said, "Oh, I give thanks to him every day. Or perhaps I should say, I give thanks to his secretary who now has to put up with him. At this point, I only need to put up with his money!" She uttered a mock sigh and put her hand to her forehead. "It's such a burden!"

Everyone laughed.

Vanessa was not amused. This did not go as planned. Kimberly was supposed to be embarrassed. Now Vanessa had to quickly regroup.

She wasn't quick enough. Kimberly continued. "I see that the desk brought in an unexpected twenty thousand dollars in revenue for the month. That's wonderful! Tell me, which auction company did we use?" This time she addressed her question directly to the treasurer who sat next to her.

"Rich Estate Auctions," he quietly replied.

Kimberly smiled at him then looked back at Vanessa. "Ah, that's your company Vanessa, am I right?"

Every head turned toward Vanessa. No one dared breathe.

Vanessa took her time. She needed to regain control. "You are correct," she said quietly. "The board agreed that it would be the quickest way to process the transaction. And of course, the commission was waved," she added.

"What a fiscally sound idea," Kimberly replied. "And along with the commission of course, the buyer's fee was donated back to the museum as well, correct?"

She looked down at the report in front of her, then over to the treasurer beside her. "Is that a separate line item here or is it included in the total for the sale?"

He glanced at the list of numbers, then back up at Vanessa. All she had given him was the receipt from the sale. It was the exact amount that had been bid. That's all he had recorded. He was about to explain this when Vanessa blurted out, "It isn't recorded yet. Separate transaction," she sputtered. "It will be on the next month's report."

"I see," Kimberly murmured.

Vanessa shuffled her papers quickly and moved on to the next item on the agenda.

Dulcie caught Kimberly's eye and mouthed, '*Wow!*'

Kimberly suppressed a smile and pursed her lips into a silent, '*Shhh!*'

Neither dared look at the other until the meeting was over.

As everyone stood from their seats, Dulcie made small talk with the board members near her as they put on their coats. She noticed that Vanessa cut short any conversation directed toward her and exited the room quickly. As the others drifted out, Kimberly remained, still chatting with the treasurer. Finally, he left as well. Kimberly turned to Dulcie and was about to speak when Dulcie held up her hand, stopping Kimberly. Dulcie turned to a phone in the corner of the room, picked up the receiver and pressed a button. "Has Cruella departed?" Kimberly heard her say. Dulcie then laughed and added, "Good riddance!" She put down the phone again.

"Sorry," she said to Kimberly. "Had to double-check that she wasn't still lurking."

Kimberly grinned. "Very smart. Shall we get a coffee?" she asked.

"Or something stronger?" Dulcie joked.

They wound their way down the stairs and through the hallways to Dulcie's office. Rachel popped her head in before they had even been able to sit. "Coffee?" she asked.

"You read my mind!" Dulcie said.

Rachel disappeared and returned two minutes later plopping down two steaming mugs. Kimberly reached over for hers and slid it across the ugly laminate table surface. She glanced up at Rachel. "How did you know I take cream?" she asked.

"Rachel knows everything," Dulcie interjected.

Rachel nodded with a mock sigh, as though it was a difficulty that she alone had to endure, then left.

Kimberly giggled. "Don't ever let her get away!" she said.

"Never!" Dulcie exclaimed. "I'll pay her from my own salary if I have to," she added.

Kimberly leaned back in her chair and took a tentative sip from the cup. "So, did you enjoy the meeting?" she asked.

"Kimberly, I thought lasers were going to come shooting from her eyes and kill you!" Dulcie gasped. "You're a brave woman!"

"I give as good as I get," Kimberly countered. "I knew she'd probably start with an attempt to embarrass me, and figured the ex-husband was the obvious choice. I was ready for that one."

"She sure wasn't ready for the question about the buyer's fee. And I don't think our treasurer had even thought about it."

"Yes," Kimberly agreed. "I think there's a reason why the treasurer is a *retired* accountant. And don't think I won't follow up on it in next month's meeting."

"Now you're terrifying me because I know that you will!" Dulcie said. "I'm glad you called her out though. She needs to know that she can't just waltz in and take over."

"And yet, that's exactly what she did, right? Is there anything you can do now?" Kimberly asked.

"Not really. Technically, I work for the board which means that she's more or less my boss. They hire the director, which would be me, then I'm given mostly free reign to run everything else," Dulcie explained.

"Is that official or just an unwritten agreement?" Kimberly asked.

Dulcie sat back in her chair. She knew what Kimberly was getting at. "Good point. I need to re-read my contract. And a few other things, too."

"Do it quickly," Kimberly suggested. "If nothing's in writing, let's put our heads together and figure out how we can get it down on paper. I'm certain I can get enough board members on my side to make it official. They all clearly approve of you and everything you've done."

"I'd hoped that was the case," Dulcie said. "Glad to have it confirmed though."

Kimberly put down her coffee, examining the table in front of her. "Lovely," she commented wryly.

Dulcie only groaned.

Kimberly looked around the room. "What's next?" she asked.

"How did you know?" Dulcie asked but didn't wait for an answer. She gestured behind her. "The armoire," she clarified.

"Interesting," Kimberly replied. "Well, I wouldn't count on that going quite so quickly as the desk," she said.

Dulcie sat forward again. "Why do you think that?" she asked.

A slow smile made its way across Kimberly's face. "She's trying to figure out how to keep that buyer's fee," she smirked. "Don't think she's selling off things just to help the museum's bottom line. No, she's making a tidy profit. That's why she's insinuated herself so quickly in the first place. She saw a sitting duck. And furthermore, she started with your office for a reason. It's a power play."

"Wow, you're good!" Dulcie exclaimed.

"This ain't my first rodeo, honey," Kimberly grinned. She demurely brought her cup to her lips with her pinky finger extended and sipped what was left of her coffee.

"Remind me to always keep you on my side!" Dulcie laughed.

"No worries there," Kimberly answered. She put down her now empty mug and picked up her purse from the floor beside her, and rummaged through it.

Handing Dulcie a card she said, "That's my personal cell number. I didn't put it on the official board list for obvious reasons. Feel free to use it any time."

"Happily! Thank you!" Dulcie replied.

Kimberly stood. "All righty then. Let's get to work! You go through your contract and see what's there regarding your duties and your staff. Let me know as soon as you can, then we'll come up with some specific verbiage to insert if needed. We can pull it together before the next meeting. I'll make sure we have enough votes to pass an official change."

Dulcie looked at her gratefully. "You have no idea how glad I am that you're here!"

Kimberly's infectious laugh once again bubbled through the room. "Oh, believe me, I'm enjoying myself immensely!" She winked at Dulcie and left, closing the office door behind her.

Dulcie sat quietly, finishing her coffee. Kimberly had given her a lot to think about. Unfortunately, Dulcie did not feel as though she had the luxury of time to ponder it all for very long. Something told her that she needed to move quickly before it was too late.

The truth is in nature
and I shall prove it.
~ Paul Cezanne

CHAPTER SIX

Dulcie had arrived early to work the next morning. She sat down at her ugly table. Then she stood up. Walking to one end she shoved it over several inches toward the windows. She sat again. '*Almost*,' she thought. She stood and repeated her efforts. This time she sat down, gazed out the window, and remained seated.

From the new desk location, she could look out and see Dan's boat. Or rather, she could have seen Dan's boat if it was tied up to its usual location at the dock, which currently it was not. Since it was a beautiful, sunny morning, he was out with another tour group. Dan loved taking tourists out on the boat, making his business all the more lucrative.

Dulcie shook her head silently. She could never do what he did. Not that she didn't like being on the ocean. She enjoyed it immensely and took any opportunity to be out on the water. It was the people that she didn't like. Not necessarily specific people, just too many people in general. She was an introvert, easily exhausted by groups, especially in confined spaces. Dan, on the other hand, was a complete extrovert. His job suited him well and Dulcie was glad of it.

Dulcie swiveled around in her chair and promptly banged her knee on the metal file cabinet that was now under the center of her desk. She'd forgotten to move it as she had pushed the table over. Fortunately, the cabinet was on wheels. She shoved it over with her foot, cursing softly under her breath while simultaneously rubbing her knee.

As she had anticipated, the cabinet provided for her was gunmetal gray although not yet dented. She knew that would happen soon enough and most likely she would be the culprit. Her knee might have left a sizable mark already. She pulled open a drawer and began loading it up with file folders.

It was at that moment Dulcie realized that she hadn't seen Rachel yet that morning. Normally she came bouncing in as Dulcie was drinking her first cup of coffee. In fact, it wasn't unusual for Rachel to be bringing Dulcie her first cup of coffee. Dulcie's brow wrinkled. The was strange. Had she called in sick?

Dulcie closed the cabinet drawer, stood and walked into the hallway. Rachel's desk was in a somewhat secluded corner of the small corridor, just outside the main gallery. As part of her job she often covered the front desk of the museum, greeting visitors when none of the volunteer staff were available. Her location gave her quick access to the front desk along with easy access to Dulcie's office.

As Dulcie approached, she saw Rachel hunched forward in her chair, shuddering. Dulcie rushed over. "Rachel! What's wrong?" she said, putting an arm around her.

Rachel was sobbing, rocking back and forth. She couldn't speak. She lifted one hand and shoved a piece of paper on her desk over toward Dulcie. With her arm still around Rachel, Dulcie took the paper in her other hand and read.

"*WHAT*?!" Dulcie exclaimed.

She looked over at Rachel who simply nodded.

"This is outrageous!" Dulcie continued. "Who does she think she is?" Dulcie looked at the letter again to make sure she had read it correctly. Yes, indeed, she had. It was to Rachel from Vanessa and was most decidedly a letter of termination. The letter indicated that Rachel would be given two week's pay, but ordered her to clean out her desk and leave her job by the end of the day.

"Rachel, this will NOT happen! Do you understand me?"

Rachel nodded but still looked miserable.

"Rachel, look. Consider this a two-week paid vacation because you *will* be coming back. Do you understand? She can't do this!"

Rachel pulled out several tissues and snuffled into them. She looked at Dulcie. "Yes, she *can* do this," Rachel sniffled. "She didn't actually fire me. She terminated my position. The board can do that. I'm now redundant, as my brother would say. Basically, you no longer have an assistant."

"Well she can't do that on her own, certainly!" Dulcie insisted. "The board would have to vote on it. I'll find a way to put a stop to this. Do *not* worry! Do you hear me?" Dulcie said.

"Yes," Rachel replied meekly. It was not like her to be meek. Dulcie didn't like it. As a matter of fact, she didn't like anything that was currently transpiring.

"That woman is like poison. She's a toxic substance that spreads hatred and harm wherever she goes. She needs to leave. The sooner the better." Dulcie hugged Rachel then picked up the letter again. "Can I hold on to this?" she asked.

"You can keep it and do whatever you want," Rachel replied. "As long as I never have to see it again."

"Done!" Dulcie exclaimed. "Now, since Ms. Too-big-for-her-own-britches thinks you'll be gone, why don't you just go home and take it easy for the rest of the day. Leave this to me."

Rachel nodded unhappily. She blew her nose into the tissues again. "I love being here!" she squeaked from behind the soggy wad. "I love my job. I always thought I was good at it. And I haven't been good at much in my life." Her voice was very small. What had happened to the confident, can-do attitude that Dulcie had come to rely on? Dulcie had never seen this side of her.

"There is no one better in this world for your job than you!" Dulcie informed her. She put both hands on Rachel's shoulders and looked straight at her. "I couldn't do my job without you. It's as simple as that. In fact, I could see you actually running a museum someday. I mean, you practically run the place now!" she added. It was an attempt to get Rachel to smile and it worked, if only briefly.

"Thank you," Rachel stammered. "I'll try to think of something to do to take my mind off this."

"What I want you to do is go home and rest," Dulcie said. "This is a shock and you need to get beyond it. Today is Friday, so relax and have a quiet weekend. Go take a long walk on the beach. Visit your brother. I'll talk to you before Monday, at which point I'll have a plan in place. Okay?"

Rachel nodded. She threw the wet tissues in the trash, then pulled out several more clean ones. "Should I throw my things in a box, so it looks like I left?" she asked.

"Good idea," Dulcie said. "I'll give you the box that I just emptied." She hurried into her office, grabbed the box from her desk, then hurried back out to Rachel. "Here you go."

Dulcie watched Rachel clean out one drawer then said, "Hey, I have a great idea! Once you're done, give the box to me. I'll stick it in the armoire in my office so you won't need to cart everything home, then back again. Vanessa will never even see it there."

Rachel brightened visibly. "It would feel like I'm not totally gone if my stuff is still here," she reasoned.

"Absolutely!" Dulcie said. She stepped back from Rachel's desk. "All right. Not a moment to lose. Are you reasonably okay now?" she asked.

"Yes. I'm good," Rachel said simply. She had stopped crying and the old look of determination that Dulcie knew so well had crept back into her eyes.

"Excellent," Dulcie replied. "When you're done, just leave the box behind the desk and I'll grab it later. Meanwhile, I'm going to rack my brain to figure out a strategy. That woman must be stopped." With that, Dulcie turned and marched back into her office.

She shut the door behind her. She wanted to scream. Who did this woman think she was? And what was her end game? What did she actually want to achieve? Dulcie knew that Rachel was only a pawn, so who was Vanessa really after? Or was her strategy to simply destabilize everything so that she could then restructure with herself at the top? That didn't seem realistic. She was already at the top. Yet Dulcie could sense that Vanessa didn't feel secure in her position. She had appeared, and ascended, so quickly. Something was amiss and Dulcie was determined to learn what that was. Vanessa had to have a weakness, somewhere.

Dulcie picked up her cell phone from the ugly table which she couldn't bring herself to call a desk and went over to the window. She opened it to let in the fresh morning air. As she breathed deeply, she looked down at her phone, scrolling through her contacts. She had already entered Kimberly's cell phone number. She located it and pressed the call button.

"I was wondering how long it would take for you to call me," Kimberly said.

"Wha...?" Dulcie began.

"I just opened my email about five minutes ago and saw one from our dear friend Cruella informing us of staffing changes that required board approval," Kimberly said. "She's called a special session for Monday."

"Are you serious?" Dulcie replied. "Did she say she was eliminating Rachel's position?"

"Not as such, but it doesn't take a genius to read between the lines. Want me to forward it to you?" Kimberly asked.

"Yes. Wait! No, let's not create a trail here. Can you print it out and give me a copy when you see me next?" Dulcie asked.

"Of course. Want me to come over this morning? Or would that be too obvious?" Kimberly said.

"Call me paranoid, but I think it would be too obvious," Dulcie answered.

"Considering what transpired in under twenty-four hours, I don't think I'd call you paranoid at all at this point," Kimberly said. "Want to meet me somewhere? How about that coffee shop on the other end of Commercial Street, down by the ferry terminal? It's far enough away from the museum so as not to draw suspicion."

Dulcie laughed in spite of her annoyed state of mind. "We sound very cloak-and-dagger, don't we?" She heard Kimberly giggle on the other end of the line.

"You mean Roaster's, right? Would ten o'clock work?"
Dulcie asked.

"Roasters! Yes, that's it. I'm retired – not supposed
to remember things, right?" Kimberly chuckled. "Great.
I'll see you there!" The phone clicked off.

At five minutes before ten, Dulcie pulled open the
heavy door of Roasters and nearly ran headlong into
Nick.

"Fancy meeting you here!" he said, holding out both
arms to steady her.

"I could say the same," she replied. "I forgot this was
your hideout." She smiled at Adam Johnson who
loomed behind Nick. He grinned in return.

"What brings you to the dodgy end of town?"
Johnson asked.

"Is this dodgy?" Dulcie asked.

"Only 'cause he's here," Nick answered, jerking his
thumb back at his partner. Johnson flicked his fingers
on the back of Nick's head in reply.

Dulcie laughed at the two of them. They acted like
brothers. "I'm here to meet a friend. Want to sit down
with me while I wait?" she said.

They both nodded and headed back to the booth
they'd just vacated. "I'm meeting a new board member
in a few minutes," Dulcie said as they got settled.
"Actually, you might remember her – Kimberly, from
the master class that the museum gave last year, which
was cut short because we lost, shall we say, the services
of the instructor."

"Ah, yes!" Nick said. "I liked Kimberly. Glad she's with the museum now."

"Me too, especially as events are transpiring rather quickly at the moment," Dulcie said gloomily.

Nick looked at her quizzically.

"Our new board director has taken it upon herself to carry out some cost-cutting measures. Not only has she begun selling off my antique office furniture, she just terminated the position of my assistant," Dulcie explained.

"What?" both men said together. "You mean Rachel?" Nick added.

Dulcie nodded. "She got a letter just this morning, then cleaned out her desk. I told her to leave her stuff with me though because she will most definitely be coming back if I have anything to say about it."

"Good for you," Johnson said. He was always amazed by the amount of fight that seemed to be packed into Dulcie's petite frame. "Rachel seems like she's hard working and smart, and that's not easy to find these days," he added.

"That's exactly what Rachel is and I'm not going to lose her. So Kimberly and I need to strategize," Dulcie said.

"What's your office look like now? Is it empty?" Nick asked.

"Let's just say that my new desk looks like the furniture at the police station," Dulcie said.

"Ouch!" Nick replied with mock indignation.

"Oh, stop it. You know exactly what I mean," Dulcie countered.

"As long as the coffee doesn't taste like the station's your probably still doing okay," Johnson said.

"Which is exactly what brings you here," Dulcie replied, gesturing around her. "What are you guys working on now?"

"A birdicide," Nick said.

Dulcie's brow wrinkled.

Johnson chuckled. "Some lady came in to the station saying that someone had murdered her bird. A hawk she'd been training. We've been investigating. I even went to the scene of the crime," he added.

"Okay, I thought my life was getting weird," Dulcie said. "Wait a minute, she's training a hawk? Does she have others?"

"A whole barn full of 'em," Johnson replied. "Well, maybe not full. I exaggerate a little."

Nick was watching Dulcie closely. "Do you know her?" he asked.

Dulcie shook her head. "No, but if it's the same place, Rachel's brother is doing research there this summer. He's working on his doctorate, and..."

"Rupert?" the two men interrupted in unison.

Dulcie looked back and forth between them silently. "You know him?"

"He's Rachel's brother?" Nick asked.

"Well, half-brother," Dulcie clarified.

"But he's got a British accent," Nick pointed out.

"Yes, because he grew up in England with his father," Dulcie said.

"Well this is all getting very interesting!" Johnson interjected.

"What's interesting?" They all looked up quickly to find Kimberly standing over the table. "Well hello, gentlemen!" she added. "Haven't seen you in a while!" She looked at Dulcie and winked.

The men slid out from the the bench behind the table. Nick stuck out his hand to shake Kimberly's, then Johnson did the same. "Don't let me interrupt!" Kimberly said, gesturing back to the table.

"Nope, you two have bigger fish to fry it seems," Nick said. "Johnson and I had finished up our coffee already. Speaking of, I'll treat you two ladies." He went over to the counter, leaving Johnson with them.

"Dulcie, quick question. Do you know Rupert well?" he asked.

"Not at all," she said. "In fact, I didn't even know he existed until yesterday. Why? Is there something you need me to find out?"

Johnson shook his head. "Not really. Just trying to put the pieces together for this scenario with the dead bird. It's all a little odd."

"I can imagine," Dulcie said. "Let me know if you do need anything though."

"I will," he said, shoving his hands into his pockets and looking off in the distance. Dulcie had learned to recognize the posture as his contemplative look.

Nick returned with two steaming mugs and slid them onto the table. "Courtesy of the Portland Police Department. Enjoy ladies!" With that, he and Johnson left.

Kimberly raised her eyebrows at Dulcie. "So, I see that things have spiced up again with your handsome detective?"

Dulcie cheeks reddened. "You might say that," she said, hiding a grin behind her mug.

"Well he's a catch, that's for sure," Kimberly said. She looked down at her coffee. "And how did he know that I take cream?"

"Oh, he's like Rachel. He knows everything," Dulcie laughed.

"Seems you're surrounded by competence at every turn!" Kimberly observed.

"Until I'm not," Dulcie countered looking gloomy again.

"Ah yes, the Rachel situation," Kimberly replied. She pulled out a folded paper from her purse and handed it to Dulcie. "Here's the email from Cruella. Pretty vague, I must say."

Dulcie scanned the typed lines quickly. "It is. But you're right, the meaning is clear between the lines. Especially since we know the events that transpired immediately after. Any thoughts as to what can be done?"

Kimberly shook her head as she paused to swallow. "I'm coming up empty. The only thing I can think of is to contact the other board members and either persuade them to stand up to Cruella, or make sure that they don't appear at the meeting. She wouldn't be able to pass a vote without a quorum."

"Well, we know that the former probably won't work as no one has stood up to her yet, except you,"

Dulcie said. "And as for the latter, she'd figure out some way around that, something like delaying the reinstatement of my assistant until there can be a vote."

"That's what I thought, too." Kimberly said.

They were both quiet for a moment. "Not to change the subject, but what were the gentlemen talking about? A dead bird?"

Dulcie smiled wryly. "Yes, the life of a police detective can be an odd one. Some woman came in to the station and said that one of the hawks she was training had been murdered."

"That's unusual!" Kimberly remarked. "Does she have any evidence to back it up? It's a pretty strange accusation."

"It is. And I'm not sure what they have for evidence. It's probably one of those cases that will fade away unanswered like so many others," Dulcie mused.

"Has to be frustrating, but then we know that feeling," Kimberly said. "We do have the weekend, however, so I'll put my thinking cap on and try to figure out what we can do next."

"Me too," Dulcie said without enthusiasm. "With any luck we can stop her permanently."

"That'd be nice," Kimberly agreed. "All right, I'm off to run errands. I'll be in touch!" she said as she moved out from behind the table. She picked up her cup and peered over into Dulcie's. "Need a refill before I go?"

Dulcie laughed. "Half of Portland wants to buy me coffee!" she said. "Thanks, but no, I've probably had enough caffeine for one morning."

Kimberly walked over to the counter and set down her empty mug, then waved back to Dulcie as she left.

Dulcie leaned back in the booth seat. She sighed heavily. What was she going to do now?

❧

"Tell me again," Rupert said.

He was sitting on the couch beside Fiona. Rachel sat in the chair opposite them. She hadn't gone home yet. It didn't seem right to be at home on a weekday, and she needed to talk. Before she knew it, she had found herself driving out to see her brother.

"It all happened so fast," Rachel said. "I arrived at work when I usually do, and the letter was on my desk. Dulcie came out of her office a couple of minutes after I'd read it. She was pretty angry."

"That's understandable," Fiona said. She was feeling a little better than the day before, but her nose was still red and snuffly.

"I don't want to bother you two though," Rachel added. "You've got enough to deal with right now." She gestured toward Fiona's box of tissues and then Rupert's bandaged hand.

"Don't be silly. Nothing takes your mind off your own troubles like someone else's," Rupert said. His hand had finally stopped throbbing and was now down to a dull ache. He'd changed his bandage already that morning, applying more of the odd smelling ointment to the wound. He was glad Fiona's nose was currently not functioning. She wouldn't have liked it at all.

"She's just a horrid woman," Rachel continued. "I don't know why she targeted me, either. It just doesn't seem fair."

"Did you say anything to her to make her angry?" Fiona asked.

"Not that I remember," Rachel said. "But then, she always seems angry, so who could know?"

"Maybe Dulcie ticked her off, and so Vanessa is getting back at her by getting rid of you?" Rupert mused.

"That's possible," said Rachel. "And incredibly mean to intentionally injure an innocent bystander."

"I don't think people like Vanessa care much about innocent bystanders. They'll take them out without a second thought if it furthers their own mission." Rupert said. He stood and walked over to the window. "Looks like Esmerelda has Arthur out again today. I'm staying away from him for now."

"As you should, the little bastard!" Fiona exclaimed.

Rachel's eyes widened. "Is he the one that attacked you?" she asked.

Rupert turned back toward them. "Maybe attacked is too strong a word, but he certainly made his intentions clear. He's done with me for the moment." He glanced down at his wounded hand. "The feeling's mutual, too." Rupert sat back down on the couch. "You know, Rachel, if you need something to do to take your mind off things, you could help me with my work."

"Do you mean, handle the birds?" Rachel looked excited and startled at the same time.

"Well, maybe a little of that, but you have to learn how first," Rupert replied. "Obviously," he added, holding up his bandaged hand. "But having only one good hand now, I need help transcribing notes. I usually do voice recordings on my phone when I'm in the field, then I type everything out later. Fiona's helping with some of it, but there's a ton more to do now since I can only type with one hand."

"That's a great idea!" Fiona exclaimed. "Please say you'll help, Rachel. Please save me from the drudgery of listening to endless hours of Rupert's voice!"

Rachel saw a flash of annoyance move across Rupert's face. Fiona might have intended her comment to be funny, but clearly Rupert didn't see it that way. Rachel quickly nodded. "Of course. I'd love to help. It really would take my mind of the museum situation," she said.

"Good! Then it's settled. It'll give us a chance to visit as well since it's been so long," Rupert added. "A good plan all around."

"I agree," said Fiona. "Now if you two don't mind, I'm going to take another dose of cold medicine and go lie down again. This is more excitement than I can handle at the moment." A few moments later they heard her rummaging through the medicine cabinet in the bathroom, then she shuffled into the bedroom.

"Let's go downstairs into the barn," Rupert suggested. "Fifi can sleep. I'll show you the setup."

Rachel stood up eagerly and followed him down the stairs. She watched him skip the fourth step, so she did as well although she wasn't sure why. She was feeling better now that she had a plan, even if it was temporary and didn't exactly solve her current problem. At least it was something.

The aim of art is to represent
not the outward appearance of things,
but their inward significance.
~ Aristotle

CHAPTER SEVEN

Dulcie wasn't quite sure why she had decided to go in to the museum on a Saturday morning. She had slept badly the night before, thinking about the situation with Rachel. Now Dulcie sat at her desk and stared out the window at the dock space where Dan's boat was typically tied up.

Two seagulls were parading up and down on the weather-beaten boards in the sunshine, looking for stray tidbits of anything edible. Suddenly both stopped and looked up into the cloudless sky. Dulcie saw a shadow quickly pass over them. The seagulls remained motionless for several seconds, then resumed their hopping.

'*Must have been a hawk, possibly?*' Dulcie thought. It reminded her of Rachel's brother. His work sounded interesting. Dulcie realized that she knew almost nothing about hawks. She shifted her focus back to her desk and opened her laptop.

A quick search brought up several Audubon prints of various raptors that caught Dulcie's attention. "That reminds me," she murmured aloud. "We have a volume of Audubons here." It was part of the museum's vast collection, but Dulcie had not yet had the time to look through it. She closed her laptop and went through the back hallways to the museum library.

Punching in the key code to the room, Dulcie waited for the lock to click. She pushed open the door and turned on the lights, closing the door behind her. The rare, and valuable, materials were kept in a second room at the back which was more darkly lit to protect them from fading. Dulcie went in and located the Audubon volume. She put on cotton gloves to protect the delicate paper from the oils on her hands, then pulled out the large book.

As her eyes adjusted to the low light, Dulcie put the book on a wooden stand that allowed her to open it without overly stressing the binding. She carefully eased the cover over and looked through the table of contents. Yes, she was in luck. Birds of prey were in this volume. She turned to the first page listed.

A beautifully illustrated owl stared back at her with massive eyes. In the low light it looked almost real, ethereal. Dulcie was lost in thought, staring at the image. She didn't hear the outer door click open. It wasn't until a figure darkened the window of the door to the inner room where Dulcie was standing that she realized she wasn't alone.

Dulcie gasped and looked up quickly. Looking back at her was Vanessa Rich. "What the...," Dulcie said under her breath.

Vanessa opened the door. "What are you looking at?" she said bluntly. It sounded like an accusation. Everything Vanessa said sounded like an accusation.

"Audubon prints," Dulcie said quietly. She looked back down at the owl, then turned the page. A hawk with golden eyes now gazed out at her.

Vanessa jumped. Dulcie jerked her head up and squinted at her. "Are you ok?" Dulcie asked.

Vanessa quickly regained her composure. "Yes, of course I am. Why wouldn't I be?" She realized she had to say something to cover her odd behavior. "I thought I saw a spider on the bookstand. Hate those things."

Dulcie nodded silently.

"Is that the only Audubon volume here or are there more?" Vanessa asked flatly.

Dulcie looked back at the shelves. She wasn't aware of any others in the museum's collection. "This is it, I believe," she said.

"No use in having only one," Vanessa replied. "They're typically in sets. Someone would pay quite a bit for this to complete a set," she mused. "Be easy to ship, too."

The anger had finally reached a boiling point and Dulcie could no longer control herself. "It's all about money with you, isn't it," she stated. "First my office furniture, then my assistant, and now you'll sell off parts of the museum's collection. What makes you think you have the right to just come in here and make all of these changes? I realize money has been tight, but we had a particularly difficult winter. We can rebound from that without..."

"Without what? Without revenue? You clearly know nothing about business, Ms. Chambers. Stick to your little art world and we'll both get along fine." Vanessa's voice dripped with condescension.

Dulcie was seething but knew she had to control herself. This was how Vanessa wielded her power. She looked for weaknesses. Now she was trying to suggest that Dulcie's years of studies both at Oxford and in several international renowned museums were frivolous. She slowly, purposefully closed the Audubon book and looked squarely at Vanessa. "It's *Doctor* Chambers," she corrected with emphasis, "And I am as well versed on the business of running a museum as I am on its contents. I also know that you cannot terminate someone from their position without cause."

"I didn't terminate *her*. I terminated the *position*," Vanessa shot back. "I am completely within the confines of the law, not to mention the board guidelines on '*employment at will*', to do so," she added.

Dulcie lifted the heavy volume from the stand. For a brief moment she considered flinging it at Vanessa but decided that it wouldn't be wise. Instead she carefully placed it back on the shelf. She removed the gloves from her hands and draped them over the stand where she had found them. Her deliberate actions helped her to slow her thoughts, calm her nerves. Finally, she turned back to Vanessa. "You may be within the confines of the law," Dulcie replied. "But you are far from the confines of civility. I think you'll find that you are not making friends here, and that will increasingly make your job more difficult." Dulcie started to leave the room.

Vanessa stepped in front of her, blocking her path. "*Friends?*" she sneered. "*Friends* are never helpful. You leave my job to me," she added menacingly. "And be grateful that I can't terminate *your* position." She paused, glaring at Dulcie. "I can, however, make things quite difficult for you. So, since you mention *friends*, well, as a *friendly* word of advice, I'll repeat: stick to the art, stay out of the business, and we'll get along fine." With that, she stepped aside and let Dulcie pass.

Dulcie could think of nothing else to say. She forced herself to breathe as she walked slowly by Vanessa and through the small room's door, then out through the main library door into the hallway beyond. She continued to stride purposefully down the corridor, unsure if Vanessa was watching her from behind. Dulcie rounded the corner, then turned slightly and looked back. The hallway was empty. She now hurried back to her office, scooped up her laptop and purse, and exited the building.

In the library, Vanessa exhaled in a long, low breath. This was getting complicated. She went over to the shelf where Dulcie had placed the Audubon volume and, without bothering with the annoying gloves, pulled the book down. She quickly flipped through the pages until she found the hawk.

Its eyes seemed to burn through the paper as it looked back at her. It was as though it said, "I know. You think you have a secret, but I know!" Vanessa shook her head quickly trying to clear out the thoughts. She slammed the book shut and shoved it back on the shelf.

Vanessa was about to leave when she had a better idea. She turned and grabbed the heavy volume again, slinging it under her arm. She *would* sell it. Quickly, too. Dulcie had seen her jump. With any luck, Dulcie wouldn't remember which illustration she'd turned to when that had happened. Vanessa thought she'd covered up her actions well, but just in case Dulcie started to get other ideas, and she was certainly the type to do that, Vanessa decided it was best to remove the item entirely. Of course Dulcie would be able to look it up elsewhere, but that was one more step. Vanessa knew that most people wouldn't take that step and bother to go out of their way just to appease curiosity.

Most people. The one thing that worried Vanessa was that she was becoming increasingly aware that Dulcie clearly wasn't *most people*.

☙

Elias Rich sorted through the stack of mail on the kitchen table. Most of it still had the official yellow forwarding stickers from the post office. He wondered when that service would stop and made a mental note to check. He'd been remiss in updating nearly everyone of their new address. Perhaps it was a subconscious action, or lack of action in this case. Perhaps he just didn't want anyone to know because he, himself didn't want to be here.

He tossed each item into one of three piles. Banking or anything official in one pile. Personal in another. Junk in a third. One letter was addressed by hand. It didn't have a return address. He threw it in the personal pile and picked up the next item.

Looking at the next envelope, he paused. Something was different. He glanced back over at the envelope he'd just tossed down and realized that it didn't have a yellow sticker. The handwriting clearly indicated their current address. Both his and Vanessa's names were written firmly in small, generic looking block letters printed carefully with blue ink.

Vanessa had always insisted that that she open the mail. It was Elias who had the task of sorting, but then each item was dutifully handed to Vanessa. Elias knew that it was slightly demeaning, but he had long since given up protesting. That would change nothing, and typically brought about some sort of unpleasant repercussion. Elias liked to avoid Vanessa's repercussions as much as possible.

Still, something about the letter seemed odd. He picked it up and held it toward the window. The sun was strong. He could see something typewritten, probably printed from a computer. That didn't seem very personal.

He couldn't make out the words. The paper must be thick, he thought. His curiosity crept higher. He couldn't tear it open, even if it was addressed to him as well. Vanessa would know. He glanced at the back. The envelope was gummed, not the kind with a sticker closure.

Elias stood and went to the stove. He filled the teakettle and turned the burner on high. As the water slowly came to a boil, he sat quietly, tapping each side of the envelope against the table in a slow rotation. It made a little smacking sound with each tap, higher pitched on the short sides, lower on the long ones.

The whistle of the kettle jarred his thoughts back into focus. He left the burner on but took the lid of the kettle off. The steam billowed out. Very carefully Elias held the envelope over it. The gummed seal began to peel away.

Elias was a patient man. He waited for all of it to peel off so that he wouldn't rip any of the surrounding paper. He turned off the stove, went back to the table, and sat again. Slowly withdrawing the paper inside, he then unfolded it. "Dear Mrs. Rich," it began. That was odd. Why just Vanessa? He flipped over the envelope to see if he'd imagined his own name on it. No, there it was. The address read *Vanessa & Elias Rich*.

He looked back at the letter and continued reading.

Dear Mrs. Rich,

I know your tricks.
I know what you are doing.
I know what you are hiding.

I will say nothing, however.
I expect to be compensated for my silence.
I look forward to contacting you again with the details.

~ *The Observant One*

Elias's hand began to shake. What the hell was this? What the hell were they talking about? Something hidden? Tricks? And was this actually a blackmail letter? Why would anyone want to blackmail them? Yes, he and Vanessa had a sizeable sum of money, but certainly not enough for this. Besides, there wasn't anything secret in their lives that anyone could possibly use as a reason for blackmail. It must be a mistake. Or someone's idea of a sick joke.

He looked back at the letter and thought hard. Was Vanessa hiding something from him? He knew that, regardless, he needed to put the letter back in the envelope for her to open. But first he should make a copy. He could take a picture of it with is phone, he thought, but Vanessa might find that. She often looked at his phone. He reached for a pen and flipped over one of the junk mail envelopes to write the words on the back of it. Then he had a better idea. Their printer had a scanner as well. He could make a photocopy. He quickly strode over to the machine, slapped down the paper, and pressed the *print* button.

At that moment he heard the automatic garage door open. She was home. He grabbed the letter and the printout, hurried back to the table, and shoved the copy under the junk mail pile. Then he refolded the letter and jammed it in the envelope. It still felt damp from the

100

steam. He pressed the seal, but it wouldn't stay closed. He licked it, but the gummed edge was no longer sticky. He heard the car rumble into the garage.

Glue stick. He ran to one of the kitchen drawers and yanked it open, stirring the contents until he found the glue stick. Thank god he always liked to have one. You never knew when it would come in handy. He popped it open and smeared glue on the flap of the envelope, then pressed it shut. He dropped the glue stick back in the drawer and shoved it closed with his hip.

Elias ran back to the table as he heard the car door slam. He slid his thumb over the envelope seal one last time to make sure it was smooth, winced as his quick motion caused a tiny papercut, then shoved the envelope into the middle of the personal mail pile.

The kitchen door opened. With his heart still pounding, Elias tried to appear calm. He glanced up at Vanessa and grunted a quick greeting. He didn't dare speak as she might detect that he was a little out of breath. Elias looked down at the next piece of unsorted mail, then tossed it into the junk pile.

"What are you doing, you moron," Vanessa said. "That's not junk. That's a bank statement." She picked it up and put it in the official correspondence pile. He grunted another response and finished sorting. Vanessa scooped up the personal pile and the official one, then went into her office and closed the door.

Elias finally breathed, a long, low inhale followed by an even longer exhale. He forced himself to do that three more times. For a moment he had thought she would take the junk mail too. He fished through it until he found the printout, then folded it carefully and put it in his shirt pocket.

He stood and looked over at the stove. The cover was still off the teakettle and there was a sticky line on the counter where he'd hastily used the glue stick. He cleaned up the glue, replaced the teakettle cover, and turned on the burner again. The water in the kettle was still hot, so it whistled quickly.

"Elias!" he heard Vanessa shout. He took a deep breath, thinking that she had opened the letter. How should he react? Did she detect that it had already been opened? "*ELIAS!*" he heard again, more loudly this time.

He went to the office door and opened it slightly.

Vanessa swiveled around in her antique desk chair. It was a heavy oak stained a dark color to match her equally heavy and dark roll-top desk. "Are you making tea?" she barked.

"Yes," Elias replied. "Would you like some?"

"Earl Gray," she ordered.

Elias made a quick exit. He located her mug in the cupboard, unwrapped a tea bag and poured the boiling water over it. As he did, he noticed that the kettle was now nearly empty. He hadn't filled it again after steaming the envelope. Of course Vanessa would take the last of the hot water. Whether intentionally or not, she always took everything. He suspected most of it was, in fact, intentional. While her tea brewed, he refilled the kettle and turned the burner back on.

Carefully carrying the tea across the kitchen, he tapped on the door of Vanessa's office, waited a moment, then pushed it open. She required that he always announce his entrance by knocking first unless she specifically called for him. He'd learned to knock after suffering her wrath on two separate occasions. Balancing the tea, Elias softly walked across the office and put down the mug. "Hmpf," Vanessa croaked. It was her version of thanks.

Elias glanced over at the desk. He saw that the letter he'd read had been ripped open with her sharp opener across the top. '*Good*,' he thought. The seal had held. With luck she hadn't noticed anything was amiss. He saw the letter on her desk, carefully folded so that its contents were hidden.

Elias turned away, but as he did, he saw her reach out for the tea. Her hand was shaking.

I paint flowers so they will not die.
~ Frida Kahlo

CHAPTER EIGHT

Fiona woke the next morning to the sound of quiet pattering on the window. She opened her eyes and lifted her head off the pillow. A soft rain drummed against the glass in the morning light.

She looked over at Rupert. He was snuggled under the heavy, warm quilt, gently snoring. His bandaged hand stuck out awkwardly as it rested on the pillow beside his nose.

Dropping her head back on the pillow Fiona realized that she felt better. She wanted to stretch her legs but feared she'd disturb Rupert. He needed to sleep. Perhaps a quick walk out in the gentle rain would do her sinuses good. The damp air would feel lovely to breathe.

Ten minutes later, Fiona slid open the large barn door and slowly inhaled in the moist air. It did feel good. She flipped her hood up over her head, stepped into the rain, and quietly slid the door closed behind her, ignoring the squawk from one of the birds. Clearly they were expecting to be fed. '*Nope, not my job,*' thought Fiona. The sooner they were done with those damned birds, the better.

She ambled along the driveway, then turned onto a path through the woods. She was glad she'd pulled on her rubber Wellies instead of her sneakers. Her feet would have been soaked already by the heavy wet grass. In the distance Fiona could see the sky brightening. The rain had already begun to subside.

Fiona thought about the birds. She didn't hate them really, she just didn't like them. They made her uncomfortable. And now they seemed dangerous, too. Rupert could attest to that. Fiona shuddered and slid her hands deeply into her pockets.

She knew it was selfish, but Fiona was glad that Rachel had agreed to help Rupert with his work. Fiona would have stepped in to assist, anything to keep his work from stalling, but it would have been a tedious chore for her. Rachel seemed almost excited to take part. Whether it was a need for a distraction or a genuine interest in her brother's work, Fiona didn't care. She just knew that she didn't have to do it.

The rain suddenly stopped and, almost as quickly, the sun began to emerge. Fiona reached a clearing and slowed, sliding down her hood onto her back. The mist around her seemed to be bathed in an odd, yellow light. She pulled one hand out of her pocket and brushed it over a tuft of tall, wet grass, feeling it tickle on her palm.

Rupert woke with a start and realized he was alone in bed. "Fifi?" he called out, but heard only the faint squawk of birds downstairs in the barn. He sat up, located his slippers on the floor and, sliding them on, went out into the kitchen. He was about to put the kettle on when there was a scream from outside. He knew instantly it was Fiona.

"Rupert!" she screamed from the driveway as she ran toward the barn. She saw him appear upstairs in the window. He took one look at her and disappeared again. Fiona shoved the barn door open as Rupert came racing down the stairs. The squawking din from the hawks, now sensing something was amiss, was nearly deafening.

"Outside!" Rupert yelled to Fiona over the cacophony.

Fiona's lungs were heaving now, and she began coughing. She followed Rupert out of the barn. As he yanked the heavy door closed, she tried to speak. "Rupert... in the woods, no, the clearing... a woman...," she couldn't think straight.

"Show me," Rupert said.

Fiona turned and began running back along the trail. She heard Rupert's heavy footsteps behind her. They reached the clearing and Fiona stopped. The woman was still there. She pointed.

Rupert moved slowly. His slippers were now soaked and squelched in the grass as he approached the woman. He walked around her, trying to see her face. He knew he should check to see if she was dead, to press his fingers on her throat to see if there was any hint of a pulse, but he couldn't bring himself to touch her. Instead, he knelt down beside her, then pulled out his cell phone and dialed.

"Shouldn't we help her?" Fiona squeaked. She was hoping, beyond hope, that she wasn't staring at a dead woman.

Rupert looked up at Fiona and was about to say something when he heard a voice on the phone. "Yes, we've just discovered a body, I think. Well, it is a body, of a woman, and I think she's dead, but I don't dare touch her," he knew he was rambling now.

Fiona felt like the mist was closing in around her. Nausea ascended in thundering waves from her stomach up through her body. She sat down heavily not even noticing that the wet, spongy soil instantly soaked through her jeans. She heard Rupert describing to the person on the phone where they were. Everything began to spin around Fiona in tight, cascading circles.

Johnson knew exactly where to go the moment he heard the description of where the body was located. He and Nick now tromped along the path toward the clearing. Nick looked over at Johnson as they emerged from the trees. He didn't have to ask. He could tell from Johnson's face. It was the exact spot where the bird had been. The "murdered hawk" as Esmerelda Graves had called it.

A uniformed officer hurried toward them. "Deceased," he said with little emotion, confirming the obvious.

"Cause of death?" Johnson asked.

"We aren't certain yet, sir," the man said. "The coroner isn't here yet. She does have a gash on her wrist that looks like it bled a lot. Maybe that? Could have bled out enough to...."

Johnson nodded, effectively cutting him off. A police photographer moved around the body, the flash from the camera reflecting for brief milliseconds in the remains of the mist that still hovered over the grass.

"Any ID yet?" Nick asked.

The officer shook his head. "They found the body," he pointed over to the side of the clearing. "Don't have their statements yet," he added.

Johnson looked over and recognized Rupert. "Interesting," Nick heard him say under his breath.

"We'll get their statements," Nick told the officer. "You can carry on. Don't move the body until we've had a chance to look," he added.

Nick and Johnson walked across the clearing toward Rupert and Fiona. She was sitting on the grass. He was kneeling beside her with one arm around her while intently watching everyone else. He looked up as they approached and quickly stood.

"We meet again," Johnson said. He held out his hand to shake Rupert's. He extended his but realized that it was useless for the task while wrapped in bandages.

"Sorry," Rupert said, withdrawing his hand. "I've had a mishap, obviously. Forgive my bad manners."

Johnson's eyes widened slightly. "Seems a number of mishaps are taking place here," he commented. He saw a flicker of fear pass across Rupert's face, but he said nothing.

"So, you found the body?" Nick asked Rupert.

"Actually, no. Fiona found it. Her. The body I mean," he stammered. They all turned and looked down at Fiona, looking very small as she sat on the cold, wet ground.

Fiona looked up at them with vacant eyes. She swallowed hard. The world had at last begun to come into view again. She struggled to stand, and both Nick and Rupert helped her up. She leaned heavily against Rupert. "I did," she acknowledged. "I found her," she added superfluously. "I went for a walk this morning. Rupert was still asleep. I've been sick, you see, with a cold. I thought the damp air would be good to breathe. I came into the clearing, and there she was. She was so still, I knew something was really wrong. I ran back and got Rupert, and...," Fiona's face began to turn an odd shade of blue-gray. Her knees buckled. Rupert grabbed her with both arms and lowered her down to the ground again. She sat with her forehead on her knees. "Sorry," they heard her mutter. "Sorry. I've never seen a dead...," her voice trailed off.

Johnson and Nick exchanged glances. Nick tilted his chin to one said, indicating they should step away so they could talk. They had barely moved several steps when Nick heard a familiar voice.

"What the hell is going on?"

He looked over and saw Rachel running toward them. She spied her brother and Fiona. "Oh, *thank God*,

I thought something had happened to you!" she exclaimed. "What is all of this?"

Nick realized that from where the path entered the clearing, tufts of tall grass and weeds blocked any view of where the body was lying. Rachel hadn't even seen it. She had only been able to spot the police, now combing through the area, along with the ambulance, waiting silently, unnecessary really, except as a means of transport.

Nick spoke in a low voice to Johnson. "Go check out the scene. We need to identify the body as quietly as possible." Johnson nodded and quickly moved away while Nick turned back toward the others. "Hi Rachel. Hold on, I'll talk with you in a moment. Could you stay with Fiona right now?" Nick asked, holding up his hand to silence her from asking any more questions. Rachel nodded wordlessly. Nick looked back over his shoulder. "Rupert, can I have a word?"

The two men walked to the other side of the clearing. "What did you see first?" Nick asked. His manner was direct. He didn't have time for conversational nuances. Nick took out his notebook and flipped to a clean page.

"I just saw her lying there in that clump of tall grass. I couldn't see her face. She was on her stomach and the grass covered most of her head. I did see her arm though. She's got a big gash on her wrist. It's weird too, because the first thing I thought of was that it was like mine," he held up his bandaged hand. "Except mine is on the back of my hand."

"A cut on your hand?" Nick asked. "How'd it happen?"

"Arthur pecked me," Rupert stated bluntly.

Nick stopped writing and glanced up at him. "Who?"

"One of the birds I'm working with," Rupert explained. "I was removing a camera from his leg. I've done it before but for some reason he must've not liked it this time. He just hammered his beak into my hand. Hurt like hell. Esmerelda had to take me to the doctor to get it stitched up."

At that moment Nick realized who might be lying, quite dead, in the clearing. "Rupert, could that be Esmerelda Graves over there?" Nick asked, looking at the other man squarely.

Rupert shook his head. "No. I mean, I didn't see the woman's face, but Esmerelda is thinner than that. Plus, she said she was leaving early this morning to head up the coast and work with another falconer today. I know I heard a car around six this morning so I'm pretty sure that was her."

"Okay," Nick said, taking notes again. He glanced over at Fiona. She was looking worse by the minute. "You should get her back home so she can lie down. I'll stop in and speak with you later if we have anything else. I've got what I need for now."

"Thanks," Rupert replied. Nick watched him return to his girlfriend. He and Rachel helped Fiona to stand up once again, and Rupert slowly led her toward the path back to the barn.

Nick turned away and joined Johnson.

"All set, Emma?" Johnson asked the photographer.

"Yup, got everything as is," she answered. "If you turn her over, I can get her face," she added as she changed her camera lens.

"Okay, let's move her onto her back on the stretcher," Johnson said, motioning to the officers nearby. With some difficulty, they managed to roll her over. In life she had obviously been a robust woman.

Nick didn't hear Rachel approach from behind him. He jumped as he felt a hand reach up and clutch hard onto his arm. The gasp that came from her was just short of a scream.

"*OH MY GOD!*" she exclaimed. "*That's Vanessa!*"

☙

Elias Rich had awakened to the sound of raindrops on the window. He lay in bed listening. He was alone. It had been a long time since he and Vanessa had actually shared a bed. She blamed it on his snoring. He had been secretly relieved.

The house was quiet. He snuggled under the covers for several more minutes until the rain subsided. Then he sat up, swung his legs over the edge of the bed, pulled on his robe and slippers, and padded his way down to the kitchen.

He glanced over toward Vanessa's room on his way down the hall. Her door was open, but the room was empty. She was typically an early riser. It wasn't unusual for her to be gone before he was even awake.

Elias made coffee. He felt strangely calm. At ease. As though the whole day was open to him and full of prospects. Perhaps he would visit the museum again. Yes, that's what he'd do. Then he'd wander along the waterfront and enjoy a glass of wine at one of the bars with a view of the harbor during the afternoon. He could watch the boats come and go. Perhaps a seal would poke its whiskered nose out of the water. A perfect day. It would be a perfect day, without Vanessa.

◌

"You have GOT to be kidding me!" Dulcie exclaimed. "Seriously, I disliked the woman as much as anyone, but really, *dead*?" She was now pacing around her living room, head down, oblivious to everything.

Rachel stepped in front of her, effectively blocking her path. Dulcie sensed Rachel's presence at the last second before nearly knocking her over. Rachel put out a hand to steady her.

"Why don't I make some tea?" Rachel said.

"Or something stronger?" Dulcie replied.

"Like coffee?" Rachel asked over her shoulder as she headed toward the kitchen.

"Not what I meant!" Dulcie called after her. She heard Rachel rustling around in the kitchen, then smelled coffee brewing.

Rachel emerged several minutes later. Dulcie was sitting, at last, on the couch although she looked anything but comfortable as she perched on the edge, leaning forward with elbows on knees, chin in her hands. Rachel slid a steaming mug in front of her on the coffee table. "I put a little something extra in it to calm your nerves," she said.

Dulcie wrapped her hands around the mug and looked up at her assistant gratefully. Rachel sat beside her on the couch, sipping her own coffee. "All right, so what's the full story?" Dulcie asked after several moments. Her brain had begun to process again.

"What little I know," Rachel began, "Is that Fiona went out for a walk early this morning and came across Vanessa, although she didn't know it was her. She ran back and got Rupert. He called the police, and of course Nick and his big buddy…,"

"Adam," Dulcie interjected.

"Right. Johnson. Did you know you're the only one that calls him Adam? Other than his wife and mother, that is. And I bet his wife calls him 'Johnson' half the time, too," Rachel speculated.

"Stay on track here," Dulcie chided.

"Yes. Right," Rachel repeated. "So, the cops showed up and started doing their thing."

"And still no one knew who it was?" Dulcie asked.

"Correct. She was lying face down in some taller grass. It wasn't until they rolled her on the stretcher that we saw her face. I happened to be standing there just then," Rachel added.

"Rachel, at the risk of sending this conversation down yet another tangent, how do you have the intestinal fortitude to stand there and look at a dead person?" Dulcie asked.

"Didn't I ever tell you?" Rachel replied. "My uncle runs a funeral home. I worked there summers during high school."

"*OH MY DEAR GOD*, this gets more and more *crazy*!" Dulcie said as she slumped back into the cushions. "Is there anything else you've forgotten to tell me? I mean, working with dead people and having a British brother are fairly large items in one's life."

Rachel grinned. "Half brother," she corrected. "And I've probably forgotten loads!" she said. "I'm just full of surprises!"

"That's what I'm afraid of," Dulcie muttered. "All right, so back to recent events. You identified the body."

"Not officially. Probably her husband has to do that," Rachel answered. "After that Rupert and Fiona went back to the barn. Rupert wanted Fiona to lie down in the apartment. She was pretty shaken up by the whole thing. Nick asked me to come back here and tell you. He said he'd talk with you later after they took care of all the 'crime scene' stuff as he put it."

"So it's a crime scene?" Dulcie asked. "Not an accident?"

Rachel looked at her thoughtfully. "Wow, I didn't even think of it that way, but that's what he said. Maybe a slip of the tongue? Maybe it isn't a crime scene yet?" she speculated.

"No," Dulcie said. "He's pretty clear about things like that. Did it look accidental to you?" she asked.

Rachel shook her head. "Not really. She had a huge gash on her wrist. It looked like it could have bled a lot.

I don't know how she could have tripped, fallen, cut herself, passed out, and then died. Especially on grass. I didn't see any larger rocks or anything like that. I'd say it was suspicious at best."

"And murder at worst," Dulcie added.

They were both quiet for a moment. Rachel finished her coffee and set her cup on the low table in front of them. "Not to be insensitive at such a sad time," she began.

Dulcie snorted.

"But does this mean I have my job back?" Rachel continued.

Dulcie had to smile in spite of herself. "As far as I'm concerned, you never lost it," she said. "I know I should be respectful considering that the woman's dead, but I can't help but feel relieved."

"You and a lot of other people," Rachel replied.

"True. She was a nasty woman. But to kill her? What could she have done that would make someone go that far?" Dulcie asked. It wasn't a question that either of them could answer.

"What I'm curious about," Rachel said. "Is why she was there in the first place. She's the last person I'd have expected to see walking in the woods."

"That's a really good point," said Dulcie. "I'll have to talk with Nick about that."

"I'm sure he'll be around quite a bit until all this is sorted out," Rachel said, trying to look serious. "I hope that won't interfere with your work."

Dulcie gave her assistant a sidelong glance. "Shut up," she said. "As you know, I am very professional."

Rachel giggled.

"And speaking of, I expect you back on the job first thing tomorrow morning. We have a lot to figure out at this point. For starters, we'll need to send out a press release. And we'll need to replace Vanessa."

"Out with the old...," Rachel quipped.

"Something like that, yes," Dulce agreed. "Last week was such a blur, but I'm pretty sure Kimberly told me that Vanessa had called a meeting of the board for tomorrow. She was going to discuss staffing changes, evidently."

"My position, for one," Rachel said with annoyance. "Although now, our biggest change will be replacing the Director."

Dulcie wasn't listening. She was thinking of how to stay ahead of this strange turn of events. She needed to speak with Kimberly. And Nick.

"All right, Rachel. For the time being, please tell no one about this, okay? Thanks for letting me know," she said.

"Am I being dismissed?" Rachel asked. She was already standing up and collecting the mugs.

"Yes, you are," Dulcie said. She followed Rachel into the kitchen. "But truly, thank you. I really was worried about your situation, and not just for my own selfish reasons. This isn't exactly the resolution I would have planned, but you're back and I'm very appreciative for that." She gave Rachel a quick hug.

"Me too!" Rachel said. "Okay, see you tomorrow, bright and early!" She headed out the door, turning on the front step. "Oh, and if there's anything juicy you find out, let me know as soon as pos...."

"Bye Rachel!" Dulcie called after her, closing the door behind her. She saw Rachel grin and hop down from the step, her untamable curls bouncing.

Dulcie went back to the kitchen. She rinsed out the mugs, letting the water flow over her hands. Strange how life had such odd twists and turns. Strange how it could all end so abruptly. Strange how it goes on, sometimes for the better, when someone is suddenly gone. That was an odd thought. Did it mean that Dulcie didn't have enough respect for the sanctity of life? No, she didn't think that was the case. Maybe some people just didn't respect the sanctity of others who were living their lives as best they could. Vanessa certainly didn't have that respect for anyone.

The water running down her hands had become increasingly cold. It brought Dulcie back to her senses. She turned off the faucet and pulled the kitchen towel off the front of the stove. As she dried her hands she thought of Nick. He might have a wealth of suspects for this case. Plenty of people certainly disliked Vanessa Rich. Dulcie herself was one of them. But did anyone dislike her enough to end her life? That was another question.

❃

The car wound along the twisting road following the coastline. Esmerelda could see the ocean from time to time, then the road would stray amongst trees again, blocking her view. She didn't notice. Her mind was on anything but the picturesque Atlantic shore.

She had just finished her work with her colleague, a falconer in Camden. He had provided valuable insight. Esmerelda was interested in using lures with her birds – balls of feathers resembling small birds that would attract her hawks back to her. It was an alternative to using actual meat. Training her birds to use the lure would serve two purposes: it would allow her to control their weight more easily, and it would provide added incentive for them to pounce on an actual victim when she allowed it.

Esmerelda had begun experimenting with a lure, but had made little progress. The bird she had used seemed confused by it, sometimes ignoring it and at other times pouncing when it should not. After her morning's session, however, Esmerelda had a new strategy and some new techniques. She was anxious to try them.

"Patience," she said aloud to the empty car. Most of the time she was a very patient woman. Yet circumstances of late had forced her to hurry her efforts. She did not like that feeling. She was not one to be hurried, and certainly her birds weren't either. It simply confused, and seemed to anger, them. No, anger wasn't the correct word. Birds don't feel anger. But they do fear, and a confused bird quickly became a frightened bird. Frightened birds did one of two things: turn tail and escape or attack. Fight or flight, quite literally.

Esmerelda thought of her own situation. Yes, this was fight or flight as well. She had chosen to flee at first, but when she couldn't escape it, fighting was the only option. The odd part was that her fight had to be a much more laborious, slow process that most would never consider to be an actual fight. Yet it was. She was fighting for everything, and not just for her. She was fighting for the survival of her birds. And to her, they were everything.

She left the winding back road at last as it intersected with the highway. Esmerelda drove for another hour in silence, thinking. She nearly missed her exit, pulling off at the last moment. Another ten minutes brought her to her own driveway. She noticed several new tracks in the dirt and, as she navigated around larger puddles that she knew were deeper potholes, she saw tromped down areas of grass on the path that led to the clearing.

Esmerelda pulled the car up in front of the barn and got out. She heard one of the birds gently whistling inside, then realized that people were in there as well, speaking in low voices. As she pulled open the barn Rupert, Detective Johnson, and Detective Black stopped speaking and looked over at her. She knew from experience that for a moment they couldn't recognize her – she stood in silhouette against the bright daylight behind her.

"Good afternoon, gentlemen. I trust you have news about my murdered bird?"

They all remained silent. Nick cleared his throat.

"We do not, Ms. Graves. We're actually here on another matter."

"Oh?" Esmerelda replied.

Johnson cursed under his breath. He still couldn't see her face clearly. The expression that someone gave when they were, in theory, surprised by something was valuable evidence. They'd missed it now.

Nick was aware of this too. He altered his manner to seem more nonchalant, hoping they could catch her off guard again. "Rupert says you've been working with a falconer in Camden this morning. How was it?" he asked.

Esmerelda walked into the barn. Her face came into view now. "Instructive," she answered curtly.

"Rupert was pointing out the bird that injured him," Johnson said. "King Arthur, here."

Esmerelda's eyes widened slightly, and she jerked her head over to look at the bird, then at Rupert. "Has something else happened?" she asked sharply.

None of the men were quite sure how to answer the question until Nick realized that she meant whether something had happened with Arthur. "No, not with the birds. But something did happen here this morning. Can we go in to your office where we can talk?"

Esmerelda said nothing but led them into the back room, switching on the lights as she did. She sat perched on one of the stools by the high table where they weighed the birds. "Well?" she insisted.

"A body was found this morning on your property," Nick began. "We are not yet certain of the cause of death. The odd thing was that this person was found exactly where you indicated that your hawk had been killed. That seems like a strange coincidence, doesn't it?"

Esmerelda swallowed hard. She could feel the fight or flight instinct taking hold. She had to remain calm. "That is odd," she replied with a slow, steady voice.

"Do you recall seeing anyone in the area either last night or early this morning before you left?" Johnson asked. He was watching her intently.

"No one out of the ordinary," Esmerelda said. "I saw Rupert last night. I don't think I saw Fiona. This morning I left quite early, so no one was up or about yet." She stopped, letting the silence drop over them. Esmerelda had no difficulty with silence. She had learned to use it to her advantage with birds and with people.

"At what time did you leave this morning?" Nick asked. He had pulled out his notebook.

"About six o'clock," Esmerelda replied. "What is this about?" she demanded. She wanted them to all go away, including Rupert. She was afraid he was already becoming a liability.

Nick thought about the timing. That fit with what Rupert had said earlier, about hearing a car leaving early. Nick focused on his notebook for another moment, pretending to read, then looked back up squarely at Esmerelda.

"We have reason to believe that there was foul play involved with the death of this person," he said.

"You think she was murdered?" Esmerelda blurted out.

Now Johnson and Nick looked at each other. Both had been careful not to reveal the gender of the victim.

"I don't recall mentioning that it was a woman," Johnson said quietly.

Esmerelda's eyes switched back and forth between them. "No, you were very careful not to mention the gender which usually implies a woman. If it's a man, people usually don't bother to cover that up since the masculine form is considered neutral most of the time. But if it's a woman, you have to work at not saying that."

It was a valid point, Nick had to admit. He hadn't considered it, which annoyed him. He thought he heard Rupert chuckle softly.

"You are correct," Nick said. "It was a woman," he added.

"Do you know who it was?" Esmerelda asked. Her voice completely lacked any sort of compassion. She simply asked a straightforward question.

"The body hasn't yet been identified," Johnson said quickly. It was true. Officially, formal identification had not taken place even though Rachel had told them who it was. Fortunately, Rupert had left the area with Fiona before Rachel had suggested it was Vanessa Rich, so neither Rupert nor Esmerelda would have known yet. Unless, or course, one of them had killed her.

"Have you ever seen people out here in the early hours of the morning?" Johnson asked, shifting the subject. "I know there's a public walking trail nearby."

Rupert nodded. "I've seen a few people on the trail," he said.

Esmerelda looked over at him sharply, then fixed her gaze on the ground. After a few moments, she looked back at Johnson.

"Yes, now that you mention it, I've seen a couple of people out hiking. Hadn't really paid much attention. I try to avoid others when I'm with the birds. It's a distraction for them. It interferes with the training."

Johnson nodded. "That makes sense," he said almost imperceptibly.

Nick surreptitiously scanned both Rupert and Esmerelda one last time. They appeared relatively calm. That could mean all sorts of things. Right now though, it was of no help to the investigation. "All right," he said. "I think we're done here. We'll be in touch if there are additional questions," he said. He turned to leave, but then looked back at Rupert. "Take care of the young lady," he said. "She seemed very shaken."

Rupert nodded solemnly. "I always do," he sighed. "I always do."

*Drawing is not what you see
but what you make others see.*
~ Edgar Degas

CHAPTER NINE

On Monday morning Dulcie sat in her office with Kimberly, Nick and Johnson. The detectives had been waiting for Dulcie when she arrived. Kimberly had also appeared, at Dulcie's request, as soon as the museum opened. The office door was closed, and they all sat on mismatched chairs around the ugly laminate table that Dulcie couldn't bear to call a desk.

"So you're certain that no one on the board is aware of the situation?" Nick asked both Dulcie and Kimberly.

Their heads bobbed in unison. "As certain as we can be," Kimberly said. "Portland tends to function like a small town sometimes."

"Does Vanessa's husband know? He must by now," Dulcie queried.

"Yes, he does," Nick answered quietly. "We spoke with Elias Rich yesterday afternoon. We had to bring him to the morgue to identify the body."

"That must have been difficult," Kimberly murmured.

"Doesn't matter how often you've done it," Johnson interjected. "It never gets easy."

They were all silent for a moment.

"Right, then," Dulcie said. "So once the board convenes, we'll introduce you two," she looked back and forth between Nick and Johnson, "And you'll do the rest, correct?"

"Yes. We'll explain what happened, leaving out as much detail as possible. I'm going to suggest that it was accidental at this point. Don't want to raise suspicions more than necessary." Nick replied.

They heard a tap on the door, then it opened a crack. Rachel poked her head in. "Want me to crank up the coffee for the meeting?" she asked Dulcie. "Oh! Hi everyone!" she added.

"Yes, Rachel. Crank away please," Dulcie said. Rachel nodded and closed the door again.

Nick turned to Johnson. "Let's step outside until it's time for the meeting. I'd rather not have too much of a presence until then."

"Agreed," Johnson said as he stood. "We'll make sure we're in the boardroom at ten," he told Dulcie. Nick followed him out the door.

Kimberly sat back in her chair. "I really don't know what to make of this," she said. She slid a lock of perfectly cut silvery hair behind her ear. "I don't know how they do it – I wouldn't even know where to begin!"

"Oddly, we've been through this before," Dulcie reminded Kimberly.

"True, but I think that was easier. Weren't there people all around the unfortunate victim at that time, if I recall? Including us?"

"UUhhhhgg," Dulcie groaned. "Don't remind me!" She stood and walked over to the window. "So how shall I handle this?" she said, changing the subject abruptly.

"As you always do. In a straightforward, professional, and gentle manner," Kimberly replied.

Dulcie spun around. "Gentle? Seriously?"

"Absolutely. You have that unique combination of being soft-spoken yet forceful. Maybe 'forceful' isn't the correct word. 'Direct' might be better. Regardless, I must say, it's quite effective – mildly frightening at times, in fact!" Kimberly said.

Dulcie raised her eyebrows but said nothing. She wasn't sure if it was a complement, or if she even agreed with Kimberly's comments. But she knew that her friend meant well.

"I appreciate the assessment," Dulcie replied. "I'll just roll with it, I guess." She looked at her watch. "And speaking of, we should probably get up there."

Kimberly nodded and picked up her coat and bag, then followed Dulcie out the door.

Dulcie lifted the wooden gavel and tapped it on the table. "I'd like to call the meeting to order," she said in as steady a voice as she could muster. Nearly everyone looked at her quizzically. "Our Board Chair, Vanessa Rich, is not with us today," Dulcie began. "I'm afraid I have some unfortunate news to report." She took a deep breath. "Vanessa was found unconscious yesterday morning, and has since passed away," she announced. It was mostly trued. Vanessa certainly wasn't conscious when she was found. Whether she was actually dead or not when Fiona stumbled across her remained to be determined.

A general gasp circulated around the table, followed by a disturbed silence. Then the questions began flooding in.

"How did she...?"

"What happened...?"

"Where was she...?

Dulcie glanced at Nick. She was uncertain what to do next. He stepped forward. Relieved, she quickly followed his lead and introduced him. "I think that Detective Nicholas Black can answer many of your questions," she said.

Nick continued to stand at Dulcie's side at the head of the table. "I know this comes as a shock," he began. "And I'm sorry to say that I can only reveal a small amount of information given that this is an ongoing investigation. Yesterday morning Vanessa Rich was found unresponsive. Emergency services arrived at the scene and provided assistance, but they were unable to revive her. She was pronounced dead upon arrival at the hospital. We have contacted her husband who is helping us to locate any other next-of-kin." He stopped for a moment.

One of the board members spoke up. "The fact that you're here means that her death is suspicious at best," he said. "So, what are you not telling us?"

Nick's face contorted into a rueful smile. "You are correct. She did not die of natural causes. That's all I can say at the moment." He looked around the table, eyeing each person directly. "At this point, we need your help. My partner, Adam Johnson," he nodded to Johnson who lifted his chin in response, "and I would like to speak to each of you individually about Vanessa Rich. No one here is under suspicion necessarily, we just need as much information as possible in these early stages."

The board members around the table bobbed their heads and looked back and forth between each other. They all had been bracing for a contentious meeting with their new director. No one had expected this. The level of nervousness in the room had only increased since their arrival.

"Do we need to have, um, what do you call it... corroborating witnesses, I guess, for when it happened?" a woman asked.

Johnson now assumed what Dulcie had come to identify as his 'fatherly' persona. He smiled gently. "It wouldn't hurt to note your whereabouts over the past day or so, and whether someone else can verify your movements," he said. "We're just trying to get a sense of everything right now. No need to worry."

Again, the heads bobbed in tentative agreement around the table. Dulcie let them process what they had just heard for a moment, then said, "Obviously we won't be discussing anything on the agenda that was previously set. If everyone is in agreement, no staffing changes will be made at this time." Utterances of approval were murmured throughout the room. "Good. Thank you," Dulcie continued. "We have coffee here for everyone and some snacks are coming," Dulcie glanced over at Rachel who mouthed 'I'm on it!' silently and winked. She put down her note pad and glided silently from the room.

"Great," Nick said. "Thanks for everyone's cooperation. We'll speak with all of you as quickly as possible. " He looked around the table. "Who'd like to go first?"

Kimberly raised her hand. "Since I've been here the shortest amount of time, I should be quick," she said with a laugh. She followed Nick and Johnson out the door to a nearby office.

Dulcie knew that they wouldn't actually be interviewing Kimberly since they had all spoken previously. Kimberly was getting her official interrogation out of the way so that she could exit quickly and talk with Dulcie again.

Rachel arrived with boxes of cookies and put them out on the side table. Most of the board members stood to help themselves. While they were distracted by the treats, Dulcie slipped out of the room just as Kimberly opened the door from the office she had been in with Nick and Johnson. Dulcie stuck her head in. "Cookies and coffee in the board room," she said. Johnson perked up instantly. He'd never met a cookie he didn't like. Dulcie grinned at him, then said, "Can I steal Kimberly away?"

"Yep," Nick said. "Are you heading back to your office?"

"Yes, we'll be down there." Dulcie said. I'll just let the board know that they should stay put until they've spoken to you."

"Good," Nick said. "Thanks."

Johnson stood. "I'll go get the next victim," he said, heading for the door. Dulcie knew he was actually on a mission for cookies. The next person to be questioned was, for the moment, secondary in his mind.

"Oh, I can send the next person in," Dulcie teased him. "No need for you to go all the way across the hall."

She hadn't even finished the sentence before he was gone.

"You had him at 'cookies'," Nick said. Dulcie heard Kimberly giggle behind her.

"Too true," Dulcie agreed. "All right, you know where to find us." Nick nodded, and they left, winding down the staircase and through the underground hallways beneath the galleries.

"I've never been down here before," Kimberly said, looking around her as she followed Dulcie. "It's like a maze!"

"Yes," Dulcie laughed. "It took me a while to figure it all out when I first came here. Fortunately, we have security cameras everywhere," she pointed to a half-spherical shape attached to the ceiling, "So if you get lost, at least you can just wave your arms, and someone will come running."

"Tell me you didn't actually do that," Kimberly said.

"No, but I thought about it a couple of times," Dulcie answered.

Kimberly slowed at a set of doors, peering in through the window in one. "Is this the library?" she asked.

"Yes," Dulcie said. "Want to see it?"

"I'd love to," Kimberly replied.

Dulcie entered the code on the keypad and heard the lock click open. She pushed through the door, holding it open for Kimberly, then switched on the light. Kimberly walked along the shelves, looking at the array of volumes dedicated to multiple topics on art and artists. "It's like a treasure trove!" she exclaimed.

"I'd have to agree with that," Dulcie said. "The real treasures are in here though." She gestured toward a door at the back of the room. "Rare books," she said simply.

Kimberly's eyebrows shot up. "Oooh! Can we see those?" she asked.

"Of course!" Dulcie led her to the door and again entered the combination into the keypad.

"Very high tech and high security!" she heard Kimberly murmur. Dulcie chuckled.

As they entered the room, Dulcie flipped on the dim light. She looked around. It was at that moment that she realized she had last seen Vanessa in this room. Her mind quickly went to the Audubon book that she had been looking at, and her eyes flitted up to the shelf where it was located. She gasped.

Hearing Dulcie's sharp intake of breath, Kimberly turned and looked at her, then in the direction that Dulcie was looking. She glanced back at Dulcie. "What's wrong?" Kimberly said.

"It's gone," Dulcie answered.

"What's gone?" Kimberly asked.

"The book. The Audubon volume that we had here. It's gone," Dulcie replied.

"Are you sure?" Kimberly looked around the room although she wasn't exactly sure what she was looking for. "Could it be misplaced?"

Dulcie glanced around as well but shook her head. "No, it's definitely gone. And here's why I'm worried. The last time that I saw Vanessa, I was in this room and I was looking at that book. Vanessa asked about it and said the museum could sell it for a good price."

"What? Could she do that without board approval?" Kimberly asked.

"I don't think so, but you know Vanessa. Approval was irrelevant to her," Dulcie said.

"So she took it, but she couldn't have sold it so quickly, could she? What day was it that you saw her?" Kimberly asked.

"Saturday morning. And you're right. She couldn't have done it that quickly, unless she already had a buyer in mind." Dulcie thought for a moment. "I need to check with security and see if the cameras show her leaving on Saturday with the book. Then we'd know that she took it."

"Good thinking," Kimberly said. "You probably don't need me here at this point. You've got plenty on your mind right now. Plus, I've had a thought. Why don't I go over to the Rich household and offer my condolences to Elias. I can ask him if he knows anything about the book while I'm there. I'll tell him I had a discussion with Vanessa about it."

"You're brilliant!" Dulcie said.

"Ah, well – sometimes lightening strikes," Kimberly mused.

They left the library and Dulcie led the way back up to the main gallery. "All right, we both have our marching orders," Dulcie said. She spoke quietly, but her voice seemed to echo around the large room.

Kimberly gave her a mock salute and smiled. "I'll report back soon!" she said, and walked toward the door, the small kitten heels of her expensive leather pumps clacking softly on the stone floor.

'That's who I want to be like when I'm her age,' Dulcie thought, smiling to herself. A security guard walked by and nodded a greeting. Dulcie remembered her mission. She quickly descended the stairs again to the lower hallway.

Twenty minutes later, she had what she needed – video footage of Vanessa leaving the main gallery with the large Audubon volume tucked under her arm. Dulcie sent a quick text to Kimberly confirming Vanessa had taken the book, hoping that she would see the message before her discussion with Elias Rich. Then Dulcie raced back upstairs to see how Nick and Johnson were coming along with their questioning.

She arrived just as the last person had gone into the office with them. The board room was now empty, except for Rachel who was cleaning up the coffee and cookies. "Wow, evidently you're never too wealthy to go for free food," she laughed. "They're like vultures with these cookies! I even saw one lady put a couple in her purse!"

"They're a bunch of frugal Yankees. How'd you think the got so rich in the first place?" Dulcie replied. "How'd things go up here?" she asked.

"Fine. Pretty low key, although it didn't take long for the snarking to start. Vanessa was not a well-liked woman," Rachel said as she crushed the empty cardboard boxes together and stuffed them in the trash.

"Yes, but we knew that," Dulcie said. "Still, you're right. Not much respect for the dead means there was even less respect when she was alive."

"That we knew also," Rachel reminded her.

They heard the doorway open across the hall and both women looked up. Nick and Johnson entered. Johnson looked over at the side table, now displaying only crumbs, with the empty boxes in the trash. His face registered dismay, but he said nothing.

"How'd it go?" Dulcie asked.

"About as expected," Nick replied. "Not much info. Most have an alibi. Of course everyone has motive if you count how incredibly annoying Vanessa was."

"Yes, but is that really a motive?" asked Dulcie.

Both men shook their heads.

"Well, here's something interesting. While you were busy, Kimberly and I were down in the library. She'd never seen it, so was curious. When we were there, I noticed that an Audubon volume was missing. The last time I saw Vanessa, which of course included an irritating encounter, was down there in the library while I was looking at that exact book. She started asking questions about it, including whether it was valuable."

Johnson let out a long, low whistle. "And it is, of course," he added.

Dulcie put up her hand to stop him. "It gets better. I checked with security, and we have footage of Vanessa leaving the building with it tucked neatly under her arm."

"Whoa!" Rachel interjected. "She's a thief on top of everything else?"

"Kimberly is headed over to speak with Elias Rich right now to 'offer her condolences' but she's going to see if he knows anything about the book," Dulcie said. She looked back and forth between Nick and Johnson. "I probably should have checked with you guys first to see if that was a good idea, but we both thought it best to move quickly."

Nick nodded. "I agree. Always good to catch people off guard. Plus, I trust Kimberly's judgement. All right, let us know what she learns, if anything," Nick said. He turned to his partner. "I think we're done here. Let's head back." Nick reached over and gave Dulcie's arm a quick squeeze, then they left.

Rachel finished wiping down the tables. She picked up the tray with the coffee and mugs. "Looks like Dulcie is on the case again as things are heating up with her handsome beau! Tune in next week as we...,"

"That's enough!" Dulcie cut her off, laughing. She opened the door for Rachel, took the heavy coffee urn off the tray, and followed her down the hallway.

ᬏ

The doorbell chimed through the stillness of the house. Elias Rich jumped when he heard it. He'd been sitting at his wife's desk, staring at the neatly stacked papers in front of him. He hadn't dared touch anything. Part of him, truth be told it was actually most of him, still thought she'd walk through the door. She wouldn't have been happy to see him sitting at her desk. She wouldn't have been happy to see him in her office at all, unless he was quickly delivering a cup of tea and about to leave. He had to force himself to sit there. Reaching over to touch anything on the desk would be the next step.

He quickly stood, as though he'd been caught in the act. Silently, in stocking feet, he padded out of the room shutting the door softly behind him. He turned to the front door of the house and eased it open.

He knew the woman standing on the step. They had met once at the museum. Unfortunately, he couldn't recall her name.

"Hello Elias," she smiled, extending her hand. "You may not remember me, but we've met before. I'm Kimberly Whittimore. I'm on the museum board, and I wanted to extend my condolences."

He hesitated for a moment. Condolences? Someone was extending condolences for Vanessa? He doubted much of her family would even be doing that, unless they thought money was involved.

Kimberly was still holding out her hand, waiting for Elias to extend his. He suddenly remembered his manners and did, shaking her hand quickly. "Come in," he said with a somewhat confused look on his face.

Kimberly wasn't sure what to make of the situation, but her years of nursing had taught her that people who are experiencing emotional turmoil could be unpredictable. Politeness tends to fly out the window. She followed him into the house.

"I was about to make tea," he lied. "Would you like some?"

"Yes, I'd love a cup," Kimberly replied. She was lying too. She didn't really want tea. But if that was what was needed to get this conversation started, so be it. She closed the heavy door behind her and followed him into the kitchen.

During their rapid walk through to the back of the house, Kimberly was able to assess her surroundings. Furnishings were tasteful, mostly antiques, she noted. Traditional colors, soft florals, it reminded her of an English country house. She wasn't sure what she had expected Vanessa's home to look like, but this seemed appropriate. Yet something nagged at her. Something was off. What was it? Then it hit her – she didn't see anything personal. It looked like a show house. No family photos, no cards or letters placed open on a table waiting to be re-read, no books lying about. It was almost as though no one actually lived there.

As they entered the kitchen Elias pulled out a chair at the table and gestured for her to sit. It was an old farm table, the sort that looked almost soft to touch after years, probably decades, of use. She hung her purse on the chair back and sat down. Elias hadn't thought to take her coat, so she slipped it off her shoulders and let it fall onto the chair back as well.

"How are you doing?" she asked him. Best to be direct.

He busied himself filling the kettle, then turning on the stove as he gently placed the kettle on a burner. He pulled out two mugs from an overhead cupboard. They looked brand new, not the mismatched, slightly chipped, well-worn kinds of mugs that obviously had seen numerous cups of tea over the years.

Kimberly was about to repeat herself, thinking he hadn't heard her, when he turned to face her. "That's a very good question," he said. "How am I doing? I have no idea how I'm doing." He stared at the floor, then looked up at the ceiling. Kimberly saw him swallow several times.

"I was a nurse for my entire career before retiring recently," she said. "I've seen a lot of loss. If this is a bad time...," she began.

"No," he interrupted. "Not bad. Not good, but not bad, either. What I mean to say is, well," he stopped, looking confused.

Kimberly stood. "Why don't you sit down, and I'll make the tea?" she said. He nodded gratefully and all but slumped into the nearby chair. He leaned forward, resting his forehead on his palms.

"I'm not sad," he said softly without looking up.

Kimberly turned and looked at him but didn't reply. She could hear the water begin to bubble in the kettle. She located a cannister on the countertop marked "TEA" and found the teabags conveniently in it. She stopped herself from smiling – in her kitchen nothing was in the correctly labeled container. If something said "COFFEE" it likely contained sugar or flour or anything but coffee. Of course Vanessa's house would never function in that manner, though.

The kettle began to whistle. Kimberly quickly removed it and poured the steaming water. She set a mug in front of Elias. "Milk?" she asked? She went to the refrigerator without waiting for his reply, pulled out a carton and set it on the table. Then she sat back in her chair, sliding one of the mugs toward her.

"I'm not sad," Elias repeated. "I'm relieved. She was a tyrant." He stopped and cleared his throat. His voice was more steady now, but still flat. "Nothing was right," he continued. "Nothing was good enough. Ever. I don't know why I stayed married to her. Maybe because I was scared of her. That's stupid, isn't it."

"No," Kimberly shook her head. "Not at all." She knew that abuse could take many forms. Emotional abuse was just as damaging as physical. More so, in come cases. The healing process was often far less direct, far more difficult.

Elias sipped his tea for several moments. Kimberly knew his brain was churning, processing. "She could ruin anything," he muttered, his teacup still in front of his mouth. "Even a simple cup of tea. Anything at all."

He slurped more of the hot liquid. "She would find out what I liked and would poison it. Every time. The museum, for example. I started going there first. I even thought about joining the board, or at least becoming a docent. But she found out. She weaseled her way in." He put down his cup. It was half empty now. Kimberly didn't know how he could have drunk it so fast. Hers was still piping hot.

"That's how I started," she said. "I thought I wanted to be a docent, but then joined the board instead."

Elias looked up at her as though he'd forgotten she was there. It took a moment for his eyes to focus. "Really? You must have a supportive spouse," he said. It was a straightforward comment although it could have been taken as sarcasm. Yet something about Elias seemed wholly genuine.

Kimberly laughed. "At this point, I have no spouse. We divorced recently. And it wasn't as though he was unsupportive, he was just unavailable. In the end we were living different lives."

"I wish I could have had that at least," Elias said, bringing the mug to his lips again. Kimberly nearly winced watching him drink and without realizing it, blew over the top of her own cup trying to cool it down. Maybe he was simply numb to any feeling at this point? Kimberly tried to refocus on her mission, the reason why she had stopped by in the first place.

"Elias, do you think Vanessa got involved with the museum solely to irk you? Or was there some other reason? She seemed quite intent on cost-cutting measures, and had begun selling off some items. The board did have some concerns that we had yet to address with her." Kimberly now took her first sip of tea, trying to appear casual.

"She did it to irk me, true," Elias agreed. "But I do know about the sale through the auction company. She never let me be involved in the business. Originally, I thought we had set it up so that we both would do it, as kind of a retirement venture. But she doesn't... didn't," he corrected himself, "Vanessa didn't like to share."

"I see," said Kimberly, although she felt as though she was still far from seeing anything. She decided to change the subject slightly. "Do you know if she was interested in birds? Dulcie mentioned discussing an Audubon book with her recently."

It was as though a bolt of lightening surged through Elias's arm. It suddenly jolted across the table, sending his mug clattering onto the floor. He jumped up, grabbing a dish towel. "So clumsy of me," he said picking up the mug which had somehow, miraculously remained in one piece. He wiped up the tea that had spilled on the floor. Kimberly noticed that he was being a bit more thorough than necessary. Was he buying time, or simply used to carrying out every task to the extreme knowing a domineering wife would criticize him if he didn't?

Elias stood and carefully placed the wet towel and mug in the sink. "If you don't mind," he said, turning to face her. "I'm suddenly very tired. I need to lie down. Could you see yourself out?" He grabbed the counter, steadying himself. His face looked pale.

"Are you all right?" Kimberly asked. Her nursing instincts began to take over. "Can I get you something?"

Elias was now shuffling unsteadily across the room toward a door. Kimberly could see a darkened hallway beyond. "No, no. I just need a lie down. I didn't get much sleep last night," he said over his shoulder. He gripped the doorframe tightly as he walked through into the shadows.

Kimberly picked up her coat and purse from the chair where she had been sitting. "All right, but please call if you need anything," she said. "I'm leaving my card here on the table." She reached into her purse, grabbed her card and put it down on the soft wooden surface. "Please take care of yourself," she added.

She saw him wave one hand feebly as he disappeared into the gloom. She left through the other doorway and was about to let herself through the front door where she had entered when she remembered the book. It wouldn't hurt to have a quick glance around, certainly. She stepped into the living room and checked the coffee table and side tables. Nothing but a few coasters and a lamp. She stepped back into the front entranceway. There was a closed door to the side of the front door where she had entered. Perhaps a closet? Silently she reached out for the knob, and gently pulled the door open. She glanced back toward the kitchen, wondering if Elias knew she was still there, but heard nothing.

Kimberly peeked through the door. It was an office. A very well-organized office. And judging by the floral drapes and furnishings, it was probably not Elias's office. Kimberly glanced around quickly, looking for anything that resembled the large Audubon volume. She didn't know exactly what she was looking for since she had never seen it herself, but she knew that Audubon prints were quite big, so this wouldn't have been a small book by any means. Nothing seemed to resemble it, though.

As she was about to leave, she suddenly had a hunch. She stepped over toward a larger armchair in the corner of the room and lifted the cushion. The edge of a large, leather-bound volume appeared. Kimberly was about to pull the heavy cushion out farther when she thought she heard a sound from the kitchen. She quickly dropped the cushion, exited the room, and silently closed the door. She paused for a moment but heard nothing more. Her heart was now beating heavily. She pulled open the front door, slipped through, and closed it securely behind her.

Kimberly knew that the first thing she needed to do was call Dulcie.

೮൪

"Autopsy report in yet?" Nick stood over Johnson's shoulder and nudged him. His partner was squinting at pictures of hawks on his computer screen. "Why don't you wear your glasses?" added Nick.

"They don't work," Johnson said.

"What do you mean they don't work? I just saw you reading earlier with them on," Nick countered.

"Yeah, they work for reading, but they don't work for the screen," Johnson said.

"So you need another pair of glasses for that?" Nick asked. He wasn't looking forward to this aging thing at all, he realized.

"Evidently," Johnson replied with more than a hint of cynicism. He turned away from the computer. "And to answer your original question, no, no autopsy report yet."

Nick walked around Johnson's desk, then his own, and sat down heavily in his chair. He looked over at Johnson who was now rubbing his eyes. "What do you make of all this? Any initial thoughts?"

"The only one that comes to mind is that it's too much of a coincidence that we found her exactly where the bird was. What are the odds, right?" Johnson said, without looking up.

"My thoughts exactly," Nick muttered. "Will you stop rubbing your eyes? Do you need some drops?"

"Ugh! Never use them!" Johnson said. He brought his hands down to the desk again. His eyes were now bloodshot and the skin around them was red and irritated.

Nick shook his head. "You look like a zombie," he said.

Johnson was about to retort when Nick's phone rang. He picked it up to see who was calling. "Dulcie," he told Johnson, then answered.

Johnson could hear Dulcie's voice on the other end but couldn't make out what she was saying. "Really? Is she sure?" Nick said. "You think she was going to sell it?" Johnson heard Dulcie's voice again. She almost sounded like a chattering bird. Funny, he'd never

considered her voice that way before. The phone must
be making it sound funny.

"... and he dead-ended the conversation? Now that's
interesting too!" Nick sounded intrigued. That was a
good sign, Johnson thought. They might have
something. Nick spoke with Dulcie for another minute
then put the phone down.

"What's up?" Johnson asked, knowing it wasn't
necessary. Nick was about to tell him anyway.

"It seems that somebody in the Rich household is
trying to hide the Audubon volume. Kimberly found it
underneath a seat cushion in Vanessa's office."

"How the heck did she do that?" Johnson asked.

"Not sure, but Dulcie said that Elias had already left
the room so, as far as she's aware, he doesn't know that
Kimberly found it. Heck, maybe he doesn't even know
it's there."

Johnson nodded thoughtfully. "Good point."

"But there's more. Kimberly sat down with Elias and
talked with him for a few minutes. He seemed okay at
first, but then she mentioned the Audubon book. At
that point he suddenly seemed terrified and said he had
to go lie down. He told her to let herself out, and it was
just after that when she discovered the book."

"Ah, so the plot thickens! Then he must know about
it, at least," Johnson said. "But does he know that he
has it?"

Nick leaned back in his office chair and bobbed back
and forth for a moment. "That's the question.
Something about it spooked him," he said. "But what I
don't get is, why would Vanessa just walk out of the

museum with it under her arm? I mean, the thing is big. She must have known the security cameras would pick it up for sure."

"True," Johnson agreed. "She obviously wasn't trying to steal it. So why hide it in her own house?"

At that moment Nick and Johnson had the exact same thought. "Elias!" they both said.

"She didn't want him to know she had it," Johnson said quietly, musing to himself.

Nick was nodding and realized he was bobbing harder in the chair. It began to creak beneath him. He reached out for the edge of the desk and stopped himself. "Why, though. That's the question," he wondered aloud.

"Maybe we should just ask him?" Johnson said.

"Yeah, somehow I think there are a lot of secrets in that house," Nick said. "Let's tread lightly for the moment. We need more information first."

"Agreed," Johnson said. Oddly, for a man with an exceptionally large frame, he was very good at treading lightly. He shifted in his chair, situating his large bulk more comfortably. After more than a decade the chair sat a good six inches lower than Nick's. The mechanism to raise it higher had broken long ago. Johnson turned back to his computer and started squinting at images of hawks again.

❧

Esmerelda Graves crept almost silently through the undergrowth. Arthur was on her gloved hand, his eyes glistening. She held the jess more tightly. She knew that look. He was alert to something.

Esmerelda had often wished that she had the same ability to have such clarity. In many ways she felt that the birds were smarter than her. Perhaps smarter wasn't the right word – birds didn't have very big brains. But they were exceptionally clever and bold in their own way. It was one of the things that she liked best about them.

Clever and bold were not words anyone would use to describe Esmerelda. Of that, she was well aware. Her latest endeavor had been anything but. She'd just managed to extricate herself before any real damage was done, meaning that her bank account had remained relatively intact. Of course then that odious woman had to turn up again. Esmerelda thought she had been rid of her, thought that her new venture would be secure in this northern location.

Taking on boarders, a scientific researcher no less, added credibility as well. That was simply a stroke of luck – to be contacted by Rupert out of the blue like that. Her hawks would be sought after all the more once they started to become known in the scientific community. She liked this business proposition much better than the last. It was far less risky.

Arthur suddenly tensed, staring up into a tree. "What is it?" Esmerelda murmured soothingly. The only time that she spoke in that tone of voice was to her birds, never humans. Arthur's feathers began to rise. He flapped his wings softly, pulling against the jess. "All right," Esmerelda said.

She let the leather strap drop. Arthur flapped his wings once, pushing off against her arm. She watched him soar up through the branches, then land on one. He remained there, motionless. Esmerelda didn't move either. Part of falconry was learning the personality of the bird, working with it as much as training it to do one's own bidding.

She heard a cry, a screech far overhead. She and Arthur looked up at the same time. "Eagle," Esmerelda heard herself breathe. Its wide wings extended straight out to each side as it rode the thermals, spiraling slowly down.

Arthur didn't wait for any more warning. Esmerelda felt, rather than saw, him sail by her. He flapped hard, fast, sliding around the tree trunks until he disappeared.

Esmerelda wasn't concerned. She chuckled to herself. It was literally the 'pecking order.' Arthur was indeed the king of the forest... until he wasn't. The eagle was a higher authority and Arthur instinctively knew this. He had no desire to confront a larger, more dangerous creature.

Larger and more dangerous. That could describe what she had gone through quite well. She thought she could handle it. It was just surveillance after all. Nothing difficult about that. All she had to do was make sure her birds patrolled the correct areas, hand off the video cameras, and collect her pay. She should have known that payment in cash meant something was amiss. At first she'd suspected drugs. Fortunately, it wasn't that horrific. However, it wasn't exactly any more legal.

Once she'd discovered that, she packed it all in quickly and left. She'd done her job.

Esmerelda cautiously, silently continued through the trees. She caught sight of Arthur once and knew he was heading back to the barn. Her footsteps led her to the public walking path, currently deserted. She continued along it, thinking. Remembering. This was where she had first encountered Vanessa. Esmerelda had been walking along, waiting for Igraine to return to her arm. She'd just put a piece of fresh meat on her glove when she looked up and saw Vanessa standing farther along the path, watching her. It was as though she'd been waiting. Perhaps she was.

Igraine had flown down then, distracting Esmerelda. She'd quickly grabbed the jess attached to Igraine's leg and rapped it around her leather glove to hold the bird securely. When Esmerelda looked up again, Vanessa was gone.

At the time she'd wondered if she had actually seen her. Perhaps she was just hallucinating. But no, she saw her again a few days later, although this time she didn't think that Vanessa had spotted her. That is, until Igraine turned up dead. Had it been intended as a warning? Was she being vindictive? Regardless, it had to stop. It all had to stop.

Esmerelda reached the barn. She could hear squawking inside. Rupert must be with the birds, riling them up by his mere presence in the cages. She was surprised he dared go in so soon after Arthur had attacked him. Maybe it was because she'd taken Arthur out that Rupert dared be among the others. She shook her head. Rupert still had a lot to learn.

Esmerelda gazed up into the sky. She couldn't see Arthur, but sensed he was nearby. She dug into her coat pocket, pulled out the plastic bag containing meat and put a small piece on her glove, then held it out. In fewer than three seconds, she heard Arthur's wings, then felt his talons squeeze the heavy leather surrounding her hand. She clasped the jess hard under her thumb, hummed to Arthur for a moment, then continued on with him, into the barn.

⁊

"So basically, the bottom line of what we're asking isn't really '*Did Elias know where the book was hidden?*' it's actually '*Did Elias kill his wife?*'." Rachel had a way of cutting straight to the heart of the matter. She didn't believe in wasting time.

Nick cleared his throat. "Yes, I suppose that's exactly what we're asking, although there are several facts to establish that would better connect those two questions."

"Such as?" Rachel replied pointedly.

Johnson chuckled. "Good question," he said, not offering any form of an answer.

Nick looked over at him from beneath a furrowed brow. They all sat in Dulcie's office. Kimberly had joined them, and she now perched on the edge of the cheap office table as there hadn't been any more chairs. Rachel had offered to pull hers in from her desk, but

Kimberly had waved her off. "I'll end up walking around anyway. I never could seem to sit for long. My mother always thought I was hyperactive."

Dulcie laughed, picturing a very young Kimberly flitting about. She quickly refocused. "So what's the answer?" Dulcie said, looking between Nick and his partner. "Do the police march over there, pull up the seat cushion and say, '*Hey, look what we found. Did you know this was here?*' Doesn't seem like that would get us very far."

"No, it won't," Nick replied.

Kimberly slid off the table and walked to the window. "What if someone else goes over to the house?" she asked. "Either Dulcie, or Rachel, or both perhaps?" She turned to face the others.

Dulcie was already nodding. "Yes, Rachel and I could go, under the guise of asking him if Vanessa had any museum records at home."

"No, we need police presence at this point," Nick said. He glanced over at his partner.

"I agree," Johnson said. "This is a murder investigation. We probably shouldn't have let you go over there on your own in the first place." he looked over at Kimberly. "Although something tells me we wouldn't exactly have been able to stop you.

Kimberly just laughed. It was Dulcie who replied in the affirmative. "You'd have been hard pressed," she said.

Kimberly walked back over and perched on the table again. "So what's the plan?" she asked. She loved a good plan.

Now Nick stood and went to the window. He could see Dan's boat docked outside. It was quiet at the moment. A seagull flew down and landed on the rail where it sat for a few moments, wiggling about, gazing down into the water. This case was like looking down through water, he realized. At first it looked clear, but everything was distorted. He needed to be more involved, to get under the surface and really see what was happening.

"Dulcie and I will pay a visit to Elias," Nick said. "Today," he added. "We need to pick up the pace."

"All right," Dulcie said. "When? And do we give him advance notice?"

"Nope," Nick replied. "We'll just show up."

Johnson's phone suddenly buzzed. He reached into his shirt pocket and pulled it out. He was developing a love-hate relationship with it and was looking forward to the day when he no longer needed to have a relationship with it at all. He glanced at the screen. "Excuse me for a moment," he said and left the room.

Nick had a feeling he knew what the call was about. He gave Johnson several moments in the hallway, then excused himself as well to join him. His partner was just ending the call.

"Autopsy?" Nick asked.

"Yep," Johnson said. He motioned his head toward the main gallery where they could speak more freely. They went out into the cavernous room and walked into a deserted corner.

"Well?" Nick asked.

153

"Initial findings are in. As we suspected, cause of death was loss of blood from the cut on her wrist. Wouldn't have taken long – it was big," Johnson said.

"That's kind of strange," Nick mused aloud.

"Yeah, and it gets stranger. No other trace of trauma other than some mild bruising on the head and hands, consistent with a fall. In other words, it doesn't look like there was anyone else trying to harm her." Johnson added.

"Huh," was all Nick could say. He paused for a moment. "So, you're saying that she cut herself, fell over, and died. Or she fell, cut herself, and died."

"That's about the size of it, yeah," Johnson answered.

Both men stared at each other.

"So how does this qualify as murder?" Nick asked.

"I know, I know. All we've got is a suspicious death based on the fact that a supposedly 'murdered bird' was found in the exact same spot." Johnson was as perplexed as his partner. He sighed heavily. "I guess all we can hope for is that they turn up something else. It was just the preliminary result."

"I can't wait," Nick said. His voice was gloomy. "There's something really strange about all this. Creepy, almost."

Intelligence without ambition
is a bird without wings.
~ Salvador Dali

CHAPTER TEN

Rupert stared intently at the screen of his laptop, watching the black and white video. He had his headphones on, listening as well. So far, nothing seemed to be happening. A few tree branches swayed, he heard the rustle of feathers, but otherwise there was no indication of anything amiss. Certainly no warning of something about to happen.

He reached his hand into the bag of potato chips and popped two into his mouth. The crunching was amplified in his ears with the headphones on. He slid one side off, annoyed that he hadn't chosen something quieter to eat. Swallowing quickly, he slid the earpiece back on again.

There it was. The crack of a twig. Anyone else would have missed it, but Rupert was an expert at listening, even for the tiniest noise. He turned up the volume a bit and replayed the previous ten seconds. Yes, definitely a snapped twig or branch. Something, or someone, else had been nearby.

He heard Igraine's wings spread, followed by the sudden, sharp noise of them beating against the air. The screen was now filled with tree branches coming unnervingly close, yet Igraine never touched them. She simply wound her way through, climbing steadily.

Rupert kept his eyes on the bottom of the screen, waiting to see if there was anything, any sign, of what, or who, had caused the branch to snap. As Igraine pulled up to the top of a tree, looking for a better perch no doubt, Rupert caught sight of a shadow at the bottom, right corner. He stopped the video, then went back several seconds. On slow motion, he played through it again. Yes, there it was. Clearly the head, shoulder, and part of the arm of a person standing in the woods. The person's arm went up just as Igraine flew by.

He replayed the sequence again. Unfortunately, the person was standing with their back to the camera. It was difficult to make out any detail. Could this be the person that killed Igraine two days later? He checked the date stamp on the video again. Yes, it was certainly two days before Esmerelda had found the bird dead.

He continued to watch the rest of the video. Igraine stayed at her perch for another minute. Rupert heard his own whistle in the distance. The bird flapped her wings hard again, making a heavy beating sound, then soared above the treetops. The next thing Rupert saw was himself, standing with his gloved hand extended. She landed and he saw his own hand grab the jess tightly. Then they walked back to the barn, the motion more jerky than before with each of his footsteps. He wondered if that annoyed the birds – it was jarring to watch compared to their smooth motion in flight.

The video ended. Rupert looked up now, gazing into the distance, thinking. He slipped off the headphones and reached in the bag again, able to crunch now without the sound being quite so annoying. Rupert finished several more potato chips, brushed off his hands, then closed the laptop and picked up his phone.

☙

Nick eyed the doorbell button warily, wondering if it would actually work or if he should just knock. It looked ancient, surrounded by layers of paint and a faint amount of fungus growth. He glanced at Dulcie. She simply shrugged. He pressed it. They heard a faint chime somewhere within the house.

"Guess it works," Dulcie said unnecessarily.

They heard footsteps. The door opened tentatively. Elias Rich peered out. At first, he only saw Nick. "Can I help you?" he asked with some suspicion. Dulcie shifted on the heavy granite stone step so that she was now in view. "Oh, my goodness!" Elias acknowledged. "Dulcie! Good to see you. Come in," He said, stepping aside now and holding the door open.

The curtains had not yet been drawn, so the foyer was considerably darker than outdoors. Nick looked around as best he could. He saw a closed door near the one that they had just entered through. '*Vanessa's office,*' he thought, remembering Kimberly's description of the hallway.

Dulcie was speaking. "Elias, I'm so sorry to hear about Vanessa. Is there anything I can do for you?" She wanted to get the condolences over with quickly.

He shook his head. Dulcie waited for him to speak, but he didn't. "This is Detective Nicholas Black," she now continued awkwardly. How do you enter someone's home, offer sympathy that their wife was dead, then get them to answer questions from the police about a book that wasn't his that he may or may not be hiding? She'd dealt with a number of social situations during her career, but this was a first.

Fortunately, they were interrupted.

"Dad? Did I hear the doorbell?" I man appeared in the hallway behind Elias. He looked over at the two visitors and began with, "I'm sorry, we've just had a tragedy, and ... Nick?" He stepped forward in surprise.

"Anderson...? Anderson Rich!" Nick extended his hand to shake the other man's. "Haven't see you since law school!" Nick was about to ask how Anderson was doing, but then remembered that the man had just lost his mother, so probably not very well at the moment. He cleared his throat. "I'm so sorry for your loss," he said, then turned to Elias. "For the loss to both of you," Nick added. "I'm a detective with the Portland Police. As you can imagine, any situation of this nature requires that we ask some routine questions. Is this a good time?

We can certainly come back later." His voice was low, soothing.

'*Damn, he's good!*' thought Dulcie.

Elias nodded. "Yes, of course," he replied. His voice sounded thin, tired. "As a matter of fact, I'm glad you're here. I wanted to show you something but wasn't sure how to go about it."

'*The Audubon book!*' Dulcie now thought. She glanced at Nick.

His demeanor betrayed nothing. '*Note to self,*' thought Dulcie. '*Never play poker with him.*'

Elias gestured for them to follow, and they entered the living room. Here it was brighter. "Sit, please," Elias said. "Let me get something. I'll be right back."

Dulcie and Nick sat on the couch. Anderson sat in a chair opposite them. "So you're in Portland now, Nick," he said. "I'd wondered what happened to you. I thought you'd be in Boston? Doesn't your family have a firm there?"

Nick winced inwardly. His departure from the family firm had not exactly been amicable. Anderson's question seemed innocent enough though. "Yes, my family is still down there. I decided to move in a different direction though," he answered.

Anderson nodded. "I can't say that I don't envy you," he said. "I went back to law school a little later in my career. It's been lucrative, but not exactly exciting. Wish I could get outdoors more."

Nick was about to reply when Elias returned. He handed a piece of paper to Nick, who read it through.

His eyebrows flew up. "Can you tell me more about this?" he asked.

Dulcie had to restrain herself. It was all she could do not to snatch it from Nick's hand and read it. She craned her neck to see if she could make out a few words on the page.

"You can read it," Elias said to Dulcie. "As long as the police are okay with that," he added, looking at Nick.

Dulcie was embarrassed to be caught in the act of being nosy but dismissed the thought quickly as Nick handed the paper to her. Her eyes skimmed the few lines on the page: '*Dear Mrs. Rich, I know your tricks. I know what you are doing. I know what you are hiding. I will say nothing, however. I expect to be compensated for my silence. I look forward to contacting you again with the details. ~ The Observant One*'

"This was sent to both myself and my wife. I mean, the envelope was addressed to both of us. The letter is just to her though," Elias pointed to the top of the page. "This is a copy I made," he added.

"Where is the original?" asked Nick. "And the envelope?"

"I don't know," Elias said. "Vanessa liked to open her own mail. She became," he paused, searching for the right word, "Perturbed if I opened it. But this was addressed to me on the envelope, so I...," he trailed off for a moment. Then he sighed. Might as well tell them everything. "The truth of it is, I steamed open the envelope so she wouldn't know. It was strange because it was addressed to us here. I mean, it didn't have a forwarding sticker from our old address. The person who sent it knew where we live now. That got me curious. So I steamed it open. When I read it, I knew, of course, that something was wrong, so I made a copy. Then I put it back in the envelope and glued it closed again."

"That was ingenious," Dulcie said. She could understand why Elias went to such lengths to avoid Vanessa's wrath.

"Do you know if your wife opened the letter?" Nick asked.

"Yes," Elias replied. "I know that she did. I brought her a cup of tea just after. It was sitting on her desk, but folded again. The odd thing, though, was that she was acting strangely, and I saw her hand shaking, as though she was frightened."

"Weren't you frightened after reading this?" Nick asked.

Elias shook his head. "Not really. I was perplexed more than anything. I mean, 'The Observant one'? What is there in our life to observe? I have no idea what it means. But obviously Vanessa didn't like it, which is odd because nothing seemed to bother her. She had a way of just plowing through obstacles as though they were simply annoyances for her to overcome."

Dulcie nodded. "Yes, I encountered that," she said.

Elias looked over at her. "I know you did, and I'm sorry for that. Vanessa only joined the museum board because of me, so it's my fault she was there in the first place," he said.

Dulcie was surprised. "Really? Why do you say that?"

Elias suddenly sat up straight. He eyed them sharply. "Because she simply wanted me to be miserable," he said a bit too loudly. Dulcie and Nick said nothing. Elias slouched again, as though that small act of defiance had knocked the wind out of him. "I apologize," he said. "We had a complicated relationship," he added. Anderson reached over and patted his father's knee. He had obviously known there was discord between his parents.

"Many couples do have complicated relationships," Nick replied in a low, calm voice. Dulcie glanced over at him, remembering his past. It had taken her some time to get beyond it. She could only imagine now how it must have impacted him. The past had a way of rearing its ugly head when least expected, catching people off guard.

Dulcie decided to change the subject. "Have you looked for the letter?" she asked. "Could the original be on Vanessa's desk perhaps?" Now she held her breath. Had she just revealed too much? After all, why would she know that Vanessa even had a desk? Elias hadn't mentioned it. From the corner of her eye Dulcie saw Nick almost imperceptibly tense.

Elias paused for a moment. Dulcie didn't dare move. Then he looked up at her. "To be honest," he said, "I've barely gone into her office. I sat at her desk once but didn't touch anything. It's as though she's still around, waiting to pounce on anything I do wrong."

Dulcie exhaled slowly now. Her gaffe had not been noticed. Hopefully.

"Do you mind showing me the room?" Nick asked. He carefully avoided the word '*desk*' not wanting to put any more emphasis on Dulcie's mistake.

"Of course," Elias said. He stood, and they followed him back into the foyer. He went to the closed door and opened it, but did not go in. Dulcie and Nick both stopped awkwardly. "Go ahead," Elias said. "I'll just wait out here." He turned to his son. "Andy, could you get me some tea please?" he asked. Anderson nodded and disappeared through the hallway into the back of the house.

Nick had already stepped into Vanessa's office. Dulcie quickly followed him. She could barely see anything with the heavy curtains closed. Dulcie reached over and slid them apart. She squinted as a burst of sunlight flooded the room. '*Probably the first time that's happened since they moved in,*' Dulcie thought.

Nick immediately began to look through the papers on the desk, trying to touch as little as possible. He was annoyed with himself that he hadn't thought to bring gloves. He pulled a pen out of his pocket and used it to poke through the papers. Nothing resembled the letter that Elias had revealed.

Dulcie was intent on other things. She glanced through the doorway to see if Elias was watching them. He didn't appear to be, although he could easily see into the room if he wished. Instead he seemed to be gazing out the window by the front door, intently watching something in the front yard. Dulcie tried to walk around casually, as though admiring the furniture. She saw the chair that Kimberly had described.

Dulcie coughed softly to get Nick's attention. He looked up. Elias had turned away now. Dulcie walked over to the chair and sat down. She could feel something hard beneath the cushion. She slipped her hand under. Yes, it was most certainly a large book. Her eyes widened. She nodded to Nick. '*What now?*' she mouthed silently.

Nick thought quickly. If Elias knew the book was there, he almost certainly wouldn't have left it and invited them into the room without him. Nick's gut told him that Elias knew nothing about it. He looked at Dulcie and jerked his head up quickly.

She got the message. She shot up out of the chair and moved to a nearby bookshelf, perusing its contents. Nick waited several more moments then turned to her. "I don't see anything here that's obvious, do you?" he asked.

Dulcie knew the question was simply for show. "No, nothing," she replied clearly enough for Elias to hear. They left the room and joined Elias in the hallway. He was still holding the letter that Dulcie and Nick had read.

"Would you mind if I kept this?" Nick asked gesturing toward it.

"I'm happy to be rid of it," Elias said handing it over. "I'll be happy to be rid of this whole mess," he added.

Dulcie wasn't sure if he meant the situation, the house, his marriage.... She wasn't about to ask for clarification. "Thanks for letting us talk with you," she said instead. "And please let me know if I can help you in any way."

For the first time, Elias smiled. "Thank you," he said. "Thank you very much. Maybe you've already been more help than you know." With that, he turned and walked toward the back of the house, leaving them alone in the foyer to show themselves out.

ᘓ

As Nick approached his desk at the police station, he saw Johnson talking on the phone. His partner waved for him to come over. Nick walked around his desk, then leaned against Johnson's. He folded his arms, waiting for his partner to end the call.

Johnson grunted into the phone several more times, his manner of an informal goodbye, then hung up. "We've got this," he said, poking a finger at his computer screen.

"What exactly is it?" Nick asked. He wasn't in the mood to play another guessing game after the interview with Elias Rich.

Johnson looked at him thoughtfully for a moment. "It's a video taken by a bird," he said, looking at Nick squarely. "Just got off the phone with our friend Rupert. He emailed this to me."

"And you knew how to watch it?" Nick interrupted. Johnson was not known for his computer skills.

The large man simply glared at his partner now standing over him, eyeing the computer screen. He ignored Nick's comment. "According to Rupert, this was taken by Igraine, the bird that was '*murdered*'," he pronounced the final word slowly and carefully.

"Huh," Nick replied. "Never saw a video from a dead bird before. Although obviously she wasn't dead at the time. So, what does it show us?"

Johnson was beginning to wonder himself whether or not this actually mattered. "According to Rupert, there's the sound of a stick breaking, as though someone stepped on it. The bird takes off, then, right here," Johnson fast forwarded through, "You can just make out someone."

Nick leaned in closer. Yes, it was definitely the form of a person. Johnson hit the play button again, and Nick watched as the person raised an arm. Then they went out of view as the bird flew off.

"Well that's interesting," he said to his partner. His eyes hadn't left the screen. "Think we can get any more clarity on the image?"

"That's what I was wondering too," Johnson said. "Let's get those tech kids on this."

Nick looked over at him now. "Uh, the majority of the tech department is my age," he countered.

"That's what I said," Johnson replied. Nick might have rapidly risen through the ranks, but Johnson enjoyed ribbing him about who actually had seniority.

Nick ignored the jab. He reached over for the computer mouse and replayed the video from where the person appeared. "Man or woman?" he asked.

"Tough to say, but my first guess is, it's a woman. Not sure why I say that, but I think it is," Johnson replied.

"Yeah, me too," Nick agreed. "Could it be Esmerelda? She's the most obvious person to be out around there."

"I don't think so," Johnson said. "I asked Rupert the same question. He said he'd probably recognize if it was her, even without the video being very clear. More importantly though, he said that Igraine would have recognized her too. And he said the bird didn't react as though it was someone she knew."

"Ah, well that's interesting," Nick said. He was annoyed, realizing that he was repeating himself. That was never a good sign. He wandered back around to his desk and sat down. "All right. We have a murdered bird who records strangers in the forest. Then we have a dead woman found where the bird was killed. We also have a letter from '*The Observant One*' threatening blackmail, although we don't know what for, and we have a missing book that isn't missing."

"Huh?" Johnson said. "You lost me on that third one."

"Oh, right! Forgot to bring you up to speed," Nick said. He pulled the folded paper from his shirt pocket and tossed it across his desk onto his partner's. It landed just out of arm's reach. Johnson groaned softly as he hoisted himself out of his chair, leaned heavily on the desk, snatched up the paper, then dropped into the chair again. It squeaked loudly in protest beneath his weight.

"You need a new chair," Nick said.

"Never," Johnson replied, unfolding the letter. He read through it twice, then let it float down onto the desk in front of him. He leaned back in his chair, stretched his arms up and laced his fingers behind his head. The front of his shirt strained along the buttons over his belly. "Explain?" he queried.

"Well, obviously it's to Vanessa Rich," Nick began, "But the envelope was addressed to both her and Elias. And it was at the current address, where they haven't been for long, so it's someone who knows them. Evidently Vanessa was a bit controlling about the mail," Nick paused as Johnson snorted but said nothing. "Elias steamed the envelope open, read the letter, made this copy," Nick pointed at it, "Then put the original back in the envelope and glued it shut."

Johnson continued to lean back in his chair. Now he looked up at the ceiling. "Seems like a lotta work to avoid the wife's wrath. But then again, considering the wife," he trailed off for a moment. "So, do we know if she opened it?" he asked, looking back down at Nick.

"Yes she did, and it scared her, if you can believe Elias," Nick replied.

"Ah, yes," Johnson agreed. "If you can believe Elias. Do you?"

Now Nick leaned back in his chair, mirroring his partner. "Don't know. He's a tough nut to crack. Clearly lived in fear of her. Still does, it looks like. It's as though he doesn't realize she's dead."

"Seen that before," Johnson said. "Old habits die hard."

"Yeah, true," Nick muttered. "Oh, one more thing," he continued. "The Audubon book that Dulcie was talking about – the one from the museum – you remember?"

Johnson nodded.

"It's still there, under the seat cushion," Nick said.

Johnson brought his hands back down and gripped the edge of his desk, then pulled himself forward, rolling unevenly on the old linoleum floor. He began drumming his fingers on the scratched surface of the desk. "Great," he said sarcastically. "So, either Elias has no idea it's there or he's creating this complete ruse to throw us off course."

"But if that were the case," Nick replied. "How does he know that we know it's there? And why still keep it hidden?" He shook his head. "No, I think Vanessa put it there so he wouldn't find it." She obviously didn't care if anyone at the museum knew she took it. Not the way she just carried it out in full view. If she hid it after she got home, she only cared if Elias saw it."

"And why should she care about that, I wonder?" Johnson queried. He sighed. "All right, let me send this," he pointed to the computer screen, "Down to the tech *kids*." He emphasized the last word, eliciting an eyeroll from his partner, "And get them on it. Maybe it'll turn up something."

"Hopefully," Nick replied without enthusiasm. "And then, let's go get a real coffee."

Johnson finished typing, paused, then raised his hand and brought down his index finger emphatically on the SEND button. He stood and faced his partner. "Now that's the best thing I've heard so far today," he said.

℃℘

Rachel slid open the heavy barn door and was instantly greeted by loud squawking. "Shut up!" she heard herself say aloud. She glanced around the interior hoping no one had heard her, but could see very little in the gloom beyond.

Then she heard someone laughing. It was her brother. "They can get pretty loud," he agreed.

"Oh good, it's you!" Rachel said. "Wouldn't want to disrespect Esmerelda's prized flock," she added. "At least, not with her around."

"I think she'd understand, although she'd never show it," Rupert replied. "Are you here to get some of the typing done?" He held up his still-bandaged and somewhat helpless hand.

"Yes, I am," Rachel nodded. "Lead the way."

They clambered up the stairs to the apartment. Rachel mistakenly stepped on the squeaky step and cringed. "That needs to be screwed down again for sure," she said. Rupert mumbled something in response which Rachel took to mean agreement. She got the feeling it wasn't a priority for him.

They came into the main room as Fiona was just entering from the kitchen. "Hi Rachel! Saw you outside. Tea? I've just put the kettle on." Fiona's words came out in one long stream.

Rachel nodded emphatically as Fiona did an about-face and went back into the kitchen. Rachel thought it was odd that Fiona hadn't asked Rupert if he wanted any. In fact, she hadn't acknowledged him at all. Perhaps it was just a given that she'd bring him some too?

Rupert pulled out his desk chair and gestured for Rachel to sit. She did as he leaned over and clicked on a few items on the screen. He'd brought up two windows – one had what looked like a video queued up to play, while the other was for typing notes. "It's pretty easy," Rupert said. "Just put on the headphones and play the video. You'll hear me talking in it. Just type in whatever I'm saying. I'll go through it all again to add descriptions, so don't worry if you've missed something. Mainly if you can just get most of my narrative in there, it'd be an enormous help to me," he said.

Rachel nodded. "Sounds easy enough," she commented.

Fiona came out just then and put a teacup down on a low stool beside Rachel. "Rupert doesn't like anything liquid on the desk with the computer," she answered, in response to Rachel's questioning look.

"Ah," Rachel said. "I suppose for the amount of work you're doing, the last thing you'd want is to have half of it ruined by tea."

"It's a good precaution. I do backups of course, but never hurts to be extra careful, right?" Rupert explained. He turned around as if to say something to Fiona, but she'd already disappeared into the kitchen again. From the corner of her eye Rachel saw him shrug. "Okay, I need to get back downstairs and set things up for tomorrow morning," he said. "Think you're all set here for a while?" he asked.

"Yup, I think I've got it," she said.

"Good. Fiona's done some of this too so she can help if you have any questions," Rupert replied. He gave his sister a wave and headed back down the stairs.

As soon as the door closed behind him, Fiona emerged again. She was sipping tea and looked far more relaxed than she had before. "Mind if I sit over here and read while you're working?" she asked.

"Not at all," Rachel said. "You've done some of this too?" she asked.

Fiona sighed. "Yes. Anything to move this whole process along." She sat down heavily on the couch. "I'm beginning to regret suggesting all this in the first place," she added.

Rachel turned and looked at her. "Suggesting what?" she asked.

Fiona laughed softly. "This whole research project. In a way, it was my idea. Rupert had been talking about this theory that some ancient human chant was based on birdsong. It got him thinking about transferring linguistic principles to bird communication."

"So he thinks that applies to hawks?" Rachel asked.

Fiona nodded. "That's what he's trying to find out, anyway."

"That was your idea?" Rachel said.

Fiona shook her head. "No, that one is all his. But Esmerelda was my idea. I'd met her before when my family went on holiday to Tortola."

"Tortola?" Rachel replied. "What was Esmerelda doing in Tortola? Was she on vacation too?"

"No," Fiona answered. "She had a similar setup to this," she gestured to the barn below, "In the Caribbean with the hawks, but I think it was less formal. She only had two or three birds there. She was training them, and we happened to be staying nearby. My mother has always been something of a birder, so she struck up a few conversations with Esmerelda."

"I never knew Esmerelda was down there," Rachel said. "How did all of you end up in Maine?"

Fiona took another sip of tea and set down her cup on the steamer trunk in front of her. She reached for her book. "That was somewhat of a surprise. I'd assumed, as had Rupert, that she'd continue her work down there." Fiona sighed. "That would have been nice! But she suddenly pulled up stakes and moved north. I've no idea why. But then, I've learned not to ask Esmerelda questions. She isn't one for small talk." Fiona opened her book, and Rachel got the hint. Fiona wasn't interested in small talk either. At least, not at the moment.

Rachel turned back to the computer and put on the headphones. She listened to the video for several moments and figured out the controls for it. Then she restarted it and began typing.

After about twenty minutes, she realized that Fiona was right. It wasn't exactly scintillating. In fact, it was mostly repetitive. Rachel's mind began to wander, and she found herself imagining Esmerelda with her hawks in the Caribbean. Why Tortola? Maybe it was a haven for hawk life? Or maybe they just liked to vacation there too? Rachel smiled to herself.

She realized that she'd missed the last minute or so of Rupert's ramblings, so she stopped the video and slid the control button back to replay it. As she did, she accidentally hit another button and another window popped up. Annoyed with herself, Rachel quickly began to close it, but stopped. Her eyes had caught a few words of what appeared to be a short note.

Without thinking, she began to read through it. '*Dear Mrs. Rich,*' it began. '*I know your tricks.*' Rachel was startled. She glanced over at Fiona, but she was engrossed in her book. Rachel read through the rest of the note and her eyes widened. She reached the end and saw it was signed, '*The Observant One*'. What on earth did that mean? Clearly it was a blackmail note.

Rachel quickly closed the window. She wasn't sure what to do. She reached down into her purse, pulled out her cell phone, and typed in everything that she could remember from the note. She wished she'd left the window open so she could be more accurate, but then Fiona might have seen what she was doing. Rachel glanced over her shoulder at Fiona again before putting the phone back safely in her purse.

Pressing the play button on the video again, Rachel resumed taking notes but was now only half listening. She wanted to finish as soon as possible, preferably before Rupert came back upstairs. She didn't want to confront him or Fiona about what she'd seen. She didn't even know which of them could be The Observant One since they both had used the computer.

Within another half hour Rachel had finished. Rupert still had not returned, and Fiona was still reading. Rachel took off the headphones, putting them carefully on the desk. Then she picked up her mug and brought it into the kitchen.

Fiona looked up as Rachel came back out into the sitting room. "All done?" she asked.

"Yes," Rachel replied.

"Good! You've saved me from the drudgery!" Fiona laughed. "Thank you!"

Rachel giggled in reply, grateful that it covered up her nervousness. "I'll see myself out," she said. "Bye!" Fiona waved briefly and Rachel quickly descended the stairs. She quietly walked into the barn but didn't see Rupert. '*Good*,' she thought. She really didn't want to get into a conversation with him. Maybe he was back in the office? She looked around as she walked toward the huge sliding barn doors but only saw the birds in their cages, their glaring eyes following her along. When she reached the doors, she pushed one open as little as possible, slipped out, then closed it quietly behind her. She forced herself to walk, not run, to her car, got in, and drove away. As she looked in her rear-view mirror, she saw the barn door open. Rupert stepped outside and waved to her. She pretended not to see him and kept driving.

*Are you really sure that a floor
can't also be a ceiling?*
~ M.C. Escher

CHAPTER ELEVEN

"They're almost sure it's a woman, larger in stature, and," Johnson looked up from the screen in front of him at his partner seated opposite, "She was wearing some pretty sparkly rings."

"Sparkly rings?" Nick replied. "That's all we've got? Don't a lot of women wear sparkly rings?"

Johnson was ignoring him and typing as rapidly as possible considering he used only the index finger of each hand. He sat back in his chair and folded his arms. "Uh huh!" he said. "Just as I thought."

"Enlighten me," Nick said without enthusiasm.

Johnson gestured toward his screen. Nick reluctantly stood and walked around the desks until he could see what Johnson was pointing toward.

An enlarged crime scene photo showed Vanessa Rich's left arm extended with two rings, each containing a large stone, stuck on the stubby fingers of her hand.

Nick remembered that the morning had been wet and misty, yet the stones still seemed to glow. "That's some serious bling," he murmured. Johnson snickered.

"I assume you've already double checked that the woman in the video has the sparkly rings on her left hand?" Nick asked.

"Yep," Johnson replied.

"Maybe we're getting somewhere?" Nick said. Hope had begun to creep into his voice.

Johnson didn't say anything. He was checking his email. "Okay, this just in," he said. He opened the message showing new results on the autopsy report. "You've got to be kidding me," he muttered.

Nick leaned down and read it. "Seriously?" he glanced at his partner in surprise, then read through the report again. "Am I reading this right?"

Johnson was shaking his head in disbelief. "Bird DNA. They found bird DNA in and around the wound site on her wrist. I've never heard...."

Nick mimicked his partner, shaking his head as well. "Could this get any more weird?"

Johnson sighed heavily. "I suppose we don't even need to know what kind of bird, right? Can they even find that out?"

"They probably can with the right sample size, but I'm with you. It's probably pretty obvious what kind of bird," Nick answered.

The two men stared at each other. Nick walked back to his chair and sat down. He pulled out a notepad.

"Ah, here it comes! When all else fails, forget the digital electronic gizmo thingies! It's good ol' pencil and paper time!" Johnson crowed.

"Shut up," Nick replied. "All right," he said, beginning to make a list. "We have a dead bird."

"Murdered," Johnson corrected him.

Nick flipped the pencil over and used the eraser. "We have a *murdered* bird," he began to write again, "A murdered woman who died from a pecked wrist, a valuable stolen book, and a blackmail note."

"Don't forget the sudden sale of antique furniture and a fired assistant," Johnson added.

"Right," Nick agreed, scribbling them down as well. He tossed the pencil down and slid the note pad across to his partner. "So how do they all fit together."

"Dunno," Johnson said unhelpfully. "But what I do want to know is, how did the bird peck Vanessa in exactly the right location, and how did she become unconscious enough to make that possible in the first place? Or did she pass out after it happened and then never came to again?"

"Which came first, the chicken or the egg?" Nick added. "It's definitely a riddle. But one thing we need to settle now is the missing book that isn't missing. That's starting to annoy me. How long do we leave it sitting there, waiting for someone to find it?"

"I'd say we're about done with that," Johnson said. "At this point, I doubt Elias knows anything."

"Agreed. So how do we get it?" Nick asked. "We can't exactly knock on the door and say, 'you have a book hidden in your dead wife's office under the chair cushion'."

"We could," Johnson replied.

Nick crossed his eyes at him.

"Or," Johnson leaned forward now. "You could call your old law school buddy, tip him off that there's a missing book, and ask him to look for it. Tell him to 'check everywhere even under the chair cushions' as it were."

"Hmmm," Nick murmured. "Not a bad idea."

☙

The next morning, Nick walked into Dulcie's office and carefully placed the large, heavy volume of Audubon prints on the ugly table that she loathed. Dulcie looked up. "There has to be a story behind this," she said.

Nick chuckled. "Very perceptive," he replied. "And there is, although it isn't that exciting. I called Anderson, told him we were missing the book, said his mom was seen on video with it under her arm, and he filled in the blanks." Nick stopped for a moment as Dulcie was about to speak, but put up his hand. "Yes, he found it under the chair cushion."

"How did you know I'd ask that?" she said.

"Great minds think alike," Nick mused. He sat down in the empty chair on the other side of the table and folded his hands. So now it seems, Ms. Chambers, that we have The Mystery of the Stolen Book to solve on top of everything else."

Dulcie had already slid the book around and began leafing through the pages absentmindedly. John James Audubon, noted illustrator and naturalist, paid amazing attention to detail. Every time she looked through any of his prints, and she had seen many, she found something new. It was as though he liked to hide little clues within his work.

Yet he hadn't simply drawn or painted what he saw. He had been a careful observer of wildlife, taking copious notes. What always struck Dulcie, however, was that although he obviously loved the outdoors, he had no difficulty documenting the more brutal aspects of it. "Look at this," Dulcie said, spinning the book around. The image showed a large bird holding a smaller one, which was decidedly dead, in its claws.

"Wow," Nick replied. "That's harsh." He thought for a moment. "I think that's what's been bugging me about Esmerelda. It's the nature of her."

"What do you mean?" asked Dulcie.

"Her demeanor. I have it in my head that someone who likes nature, wildlife, and trains animals, or birds in this case, must be a kind, benevolent person. But Esmerelda obviously isn't."

"Maybe she is, she just doesn't show it," Dulcie replied.

"Or shows it in a different way?" Nick said. "No, I don't think kindness or benevolence have much to do with any of it. Nature is matter-of-fact. It follows set rules. Kill or be killed."

Dulcie stopped turning pages and glanced up at Nick. "That was an odd phrase to use," she remarked.

"Wasn't it," Nick agreed. He sat silent for a moment. Dulcie watched him. His mind was turning everything over. He sat back in his chair. "Dulcie, Vanessa began selling the furniture here," he gestured toward the ugly table, "Ostensibly to get money for the museum, right?"

"Correct," Dulcie said. "But she also stood to make a commission on the side, we discovered. She waived her own commission so that the museum wouldn't have to pay it, but didn't waive the buyer's fee." Dulcie inhaled sharply. "Nick! She also wanted to sell this book! And she'd have made a tidy commission on that too, presumably. But what if she didn't want her husband to know about it? Does that mean she could have had money problems that she wanted to keep hidden from him?"

"It could," Nick nodded slowly. "We checked their bank accounts, and nothing seemed amiss really. They're certainly not hurting for cash," he added.

"Yes, but if she was being blackmailed, and presumably she would know who was doing it, 'The Observant One', right?" Dulcie suggested.

"Right," Nick responded slowly. "Elias didn't seem concerned, but then he might not have known anything about it."

A soft knock at the door made both Dulcie and Nick look up. The door opened and Rachel poked her head inside. "Oh, good! You're here too," she said to Nick and came in the room, closing the door behind her.

"I've got something to tell you," she said, sitting down on the edge of the table. She swung one leg back and forth nervously.

Dulcie realized that no one in the past had ever sat on her desk, yet somehow everyone, including herself, seemed to have no problem plopping down on this flimsy table. Why was that? She shook her head quickly to refocus. Rachel was talking again.

"Let me say first that I don't want to get anyone in trouble and I'm sure there's a perfectly reasonable explanation," she began, then took a deep breath. "I went over to Rupert's late yesterday after work to type up some of his notes," she said. "While I was typing, I hit a wrong key, and this popped up," she held up her cell phone in front of her, pulled up the note that she had quickly copied down, and put the phone on the table. Dulcie and Nick leaned over quickly to read it, nearly smacking heads in the process.

Nick's eyes widened. "Did anyone see you find this?" he asked.

"No, don't think so," Rachel said. Rupert got me started on the computer when I first arrived, then he went down to the barn. Fiona was reading her book on the other side of the room."

"Would they know if you saw it?" Dulcie asked. "I mean, after the fact, like a time stamp on the file or something?"

Again, Rachel shook her head. "I think I hit one of the buttons that just shows you what's in the file but doesn't open the file itself. The margins looked like they were all off and stuff. I don't think they'd know that I saw it," she said.

"What did you do afterward?" Nick asked.

"I made sure Fiona wasn't watching, quickly wrote down all this," she gestured toward the phone, "Finished my work, and left. Oh, but there was another thing that seemed odd. Fiona said that coming to Maine was her idea. No wait, that isn't quite right. The 'coming to Maine' part I mean. Her idea was for Rupert to work with Esmerelda. But I don't think she knew they would be living here in Maine."

"Really?" both Nick and Dulcie exclaimed in unison.

Rachel nodded. "Fiona met Esmerelda in Tortola a while back when she was on vacation. She said she was with her parents, so I don't think Rupert was there."

"Rachel," Nick interrupted, "Is that laptop the only computer they have?" he asked.

Rachel shrugged her shoulders. "I think so, but I'm not sure. They both use it, though. I mean, Fiona also types up some of his notes, just like I did yesterday."

Nick was now softly drumming on the table with his fingers. "Rachel, it goes without saying but I'll say it: don't discuss this with anyone." It was an order.

"Is Rupert in trouble?" Rachel asked. Concern had crept into her eyes. "I mean, he's my brother. We aren't that close – we didn't exactly grow up together, but I can't imagine he did anything really wrong. I mean, it could have been Fiona. I'll bet it was. What do we really know about her?" Rachel realized she was kicking her leg harder under the table and forced herself to stop.

"I don't know, Rachel," Nick said quietly. "But I'll look into this. Quietly. It could be nothing."

"Or it could be Fiona, as you say," Dulcie added.

Rachel slid off the table. "That must be it," she said. "There's something about her that I'm not sure I like."

Nick stood too. "All right, I'll leave you both and check this out." He strode quickly from the room.

"Look Rachel, as Nick said, it's probably nothing. Or nothing to be concerned about, anyway. Rupert isn't stupid. He wouldn't do anything to impact his research negatively. It's too important to him," Dulcie said.

Rachel nodded in agreement but didn't appear entirely convinced. "You're right. Okay, I'll get back to work," she turned quickly toward the door, her unruly hair flying outward from her head.

Dulcie sat quietly looking at the Audubon volume again. She wasn't paying attention to the pages, however. Her mind was turning over the pieces of the puzzle, trying to make them fit, yet they didn't. She hoped Nick was having better luck.

CB

Nick marched into the police station. Johnson had just sat down at his desk. "The note," Nick announced. He sat down and faced Johnson. "The note," he repeated.

"So you've said," Johnson replied.

"Either Rupert or Fiona wrote it," Nick said.

Johnson's eyebrows flew up. "You don't say!"

Nick nodded. "Rachel was on their computer typing up Rupert's research work and saw it."

"Well, I'll be...!" Johnson began.

"And there's more," Nick interjected. "Fiona first met Esmerelda in Tortola."

"Where the heck's Tortola?" Johnson asked. He stared off into the distance for a moment, trying to remember his geography.

"The British Virgin Islands," Nick replied. He said nothing more, waiting for the information to sink into his partner's brain.

"Hang on a second," Johnson was now pecking away at his keyboard hunting for a map of the Caribbean. "Wasn't Esmerelda in St. John? But that's the US Virgin Islands."

"Right," Nick said.

"So now she's also in the British Virgin Islands?" Johnson's chin was nearly on his desk as he leaned forward, squinting at the screen. "Jeez, look how close they are! I didn't realize that."

"Umm-hmm," Nick agreed.

Johnson leaned back again. "So what does this mean?" he asked.

"It means she was down there, with her hawks. And she knows Fiona. I'd say we need to talk to both of them, and Rupert. Let's get to the bottom of this blackmail note and see just who has been chummy in the past with whom."

Nick was glad to see Esmerelda's car parked near the barn. He really wanted to confront all of them at the same time. As they approached the large, weathered building, the heavy sliding door was already open.

Johnson and Nick could hear people talking inside. "Hello?" Nick called out.

Rupert appeared in the office doorway. "Oh, hi! C'mon in," he said waving them through. Esmerelda sat on one of the stools at the tall table. Johnson looked around the room. "Is Fiona around?" he asked.

Rupert looked puzzled. "She's upstairs," he said simply.

"Can you get her please?" Johnson asked.

Rupert hesitated for a moment, but then nodded and left.

"What's this all about? Do you have any news?" Esmerelda asked. She did not appear to be happy, Nick noticed. Then again, he couldn't imagine her ever actually looking happy.

They heard the two others clomping down the stairs. As they came into the room, Nick pulled out a copy of the threatening note. He put it on the table. "Does anyone recognize this?"

Esmerelda read through it carefully. "I have no idea what that is," she said. "The Observant One? Sounds strange to me."

Rupert and Fiona remained silent. Nick looked at them. "I'm not surprised that Esmerelda knows nothing about it. But one, or both, of you two might?"

Rupert cleared his throat. "Look, nothing really was intended behind it," he said. "I mean, Fifi and I were incensed that Rachel lost her job. That woman at the museum thought she could get away with anything, so we decided to scare her off a little. That's all."

"But the way it's written," Nick said. "'I know your tricks,' and all of that. Do you know something about her that we should be aware of?"

Rupert shook his head. "No. I mean, everyone has secrets, right? It's the '*I Know*' game. If you say that to anyone, they'll get nervous because everyone has something to hide, right?"

Nick didn't answer. He was watching Fiona. She had grown very pale. He saw her glance over at Esmerelda.

"That seems like a pretty dangerous game to play in this case," Johnson said. "Considering the person receiving the note wound up dead?"

Rupert looked at the ground. "I realize that, and I swear I didn't intend anything horrible. I just wanted to help Rachel. I really didn't think it through, though, did I."

"Seems you didn't," Nick said quietly.

The room was silent for a moment. They could her the birds softly chirping to each other in the darkness of the barn.

"What now?" asked Esmerelda. "Do you have no information on Igraine, either?"

Nick ignored the question. "I understand you two ladies know each other from travels in the Caribbean?" he said pointedly.

The women exchanged a quick glance. "Yes, we met there," Esmerelda said.

Fiona nodded. "I was on Tortola with my parents, on holiday. Esmerelda was training her hawks. My mother has always been interested in falconry, so she struck up a conversation."

"What were you doing on Tortola," Nick asked. "I understood that you lived on St. John for a while?"

For the first time, Esmerelda seemed startled. She regained her composure quickly. "Birds do fly, you understand," she said with some sarcasm. "I did have a boat as well, and the islands are very close in spite of belonging to different countries. People down there don't tend to think about that much. And the birds certainly don't care."

Johnson was taking notes as unobtrusively and rapidly as possible. He moved slightly behind his partner so that his notepad was blocked from view by the others.

"Are you accusing anyone of anything?" Esmerelda said with her usual bluntness.

"Not yet," Nick replied. He turned to Rupert. "I understand that you didn't intend anything and that you only wanted to protect your sister, but blackmail is a serious crime, so we'll need to resolve that. If you could come to the station by tomorrow afternoon and make an official statement, that would help your case."

"Certainly," Rupert said solemnly.

"You'll need to bring your laptop as well. If you want to even try to clear your name, we'll need to have a look at your files."

Rupert looked concerned. "Of course, but you won't need to keep it, will you? I mean, I need it for my work. I can show you the note on there. That's enough, isn't it?"

"Let's hope so," Nick replied.

"Is there anything else?" Fiona asked. "I have something in the oven," she gestured upstairs.

"No, that should be all," Nick answered. Fiona nearly bolted from the room.

Johnson made a quick note of this also. "We'll be in touch," he added as he and his partner left.

As he closed the car door, Nick turned to his partner. "Think Fiona really had to check on her baking?"

"Not at all," Johnson replied. "Doesn't exactly strike me as a cook. Or even the domestic type."

"Agreed," Nick said. "We need to do some digging on her. And more on Esmerelda. She's hiding something, too."

"Yep," Johnson said as he navigated around the potholes. "Things aren't adding up, but I get the odd feeling they're about to."

"Yeah, me too," Nick murmured. "Me too."

Everything you can imagine is real.
~ Pablo Picasso

CHAPTER TWELVE

"Is that the Audubon book Vanessa decided to make off with?" Kimberly was sitting in Dulcie's office waiting for her. Dulcie had just entered and looked at her friend, then the book, then back at her friend.

"Why yes, it is! And I'm glad to see you!" she added. She actually *was* glad to see Kimberly. Somehow the woman's presence calmed Dulcie.

"Could I glance at it?" Kimberly asked. "I don't think I've ever seen original prints of his before. Lots of copies, certainly, but never the real deal."

"Of course," Dulcie said. She slid the large volume over. "I think Vanessa intended to sell. What do you think?"

Kimberly simply nodded. She was carefully turning over the pages as though they were made of onion skin instead of the heavier printed plates that they were. "They are beautiful. Vanessa would have made a good commission."

"Yes, she would have," Dulcie agreed. She looked over at the vividly colored images. Now she saw the owl that she had been looking at when Vanessa had appeared in the library that day. Kimberly turned the next leaf over and Dulcie gasped. It was a hawk. She remembered it now, with yellow eyes and the strong, hooked beak. "Stop there," Dulcie said. "Look at that. When Vanessa confronted me in the library, I had just turned over to that page. She seemed startled when she saw it. I remember that she tried to cover up her reaction by saying something about a spider she thought she'd seen. But it wasn't a spider, I'm sure. It was the hawk."

Kimberly carefully slid the book over so that they could both look at it. "Keep going with that thought. What's your instinct? Why do you think she was startled?"

Dulcie continued to stare at the illustration. "I don't think it was the drawing so much as the subject. The hawk. That's my gut feeling." She looked up at Kimberly. "It seems like quite a coincidence, don't you think, that she would react to a hawk, and she was killed on the property of a falconer?"

"Actually, she was killed by a hawk." Nick had just walked into the room.

"What?!" both women exclaimed at the same time.

"It seems that her wrist was pecked by a hawk. At some point she passed out, and she lost too much blood to recover," he replied.

"Are you serious?" Dulcie said.

"I am. I don't think I could make that one up," Nick said.

"How is that even possible?" Kimberly mused. "It couldn't be an accident, could it?" The nurse in her had taken over again. She was thinking about the force of the blow, whether or not someone like Vanessa would faint immediately. It was difficult to tell. Kimberly had seen a professional athlete black out and hit the floor from simply having his blood drawn in the lab, yet she herself didn't seem affected at all in that way, even when she'd worked in the emergency room where she saw her fair share of accidents. It all depended on the person, so it was possible for Vanessa to simply lose consciousness at the sight of her own blood.

The part that bothered Kimberly, however, was how the bird had been able to peck the correct spot in the first place. Was that merely a twist of fate? Had someone tried to train a hawk to kill a person?

"Earth to Kimberly!" Dulcie had been watching her friend. "What were you thinking?"

"This all seems far too risky if the intent was to kill Vanessa," she mused, rather than trying to relate everything that had just passed through her mind.

"I assume you mean from a medical perspective?" Nick asked. "How so?"

Kimberly stood and began pacing on the large Persian carpet. "First of all, how could a bird peck the exact spot where there happens to be a major artery? Secondly, was Vanessa the type of person to faint at the sight of her own blood? Thirdly, would she have fainted for long enough for blood loss to be sufficient to kill her?" She stopped and turned around toward the others. "If I were planning a murder, those are some pretty big hurdles to jump over."

"That's true," Nick said. "Maybe murder wasn't the intent? Maybe someone just wanted to scare Vanessa?"

"Do you mean, Rupert?" Dulcie asked.

"Possibly," Nick replied. "It fits with what we know so far."

Dulcie shook her head. "I just don't see it. I mean, what motivation could he have? He wouldn't go that far just to scare her into giving Rachel her job back."

"Wait, am I missing something?" Kimberly asked.

Dulcie laughed. "You are indeed," she turned to Nick. "Can I tell her about the note?" He nodded, and Dulcie quickly explained.

"I'm with Dulcie," Kimberly said to Nick as soon as Dulcie finished speaking. I don't see it. The motivation wouldn't be strong enough."

Nick sighed. They were right. "The only other person that I can think of is Esmerelda. Maybe she could have trained a hawk well enough to do something like that?"

"Did she have opportunity?" Dulcie asked. "Where was she that morning?"

"She left early to work with a colleague up in Camden," Nick said.

"Then she could have arranged to meet Vanessa, brought the hawk out, let the bird do its thing, then put the bird back and drive off. Is that possible?" Dulcie said.

"It's possible," Nick replied, "But why? Again, what's the motivation? They didn't even know each other." The room was silent as the three people thought. No one had the answer. "All righty then," Nick finally said as he stood. "Back to the drawing board. Let me know if you find out anything?" he asked as he walked toward the door.

"Don't we always?" Kimberly said in a sly voice.

"Not always," Nick called over his shoulder from the hallway.

Dulcie chuckled knowing he was right. She got up from her chair and went over to the window. Dan was just bringing the boat back in, chatting with the tourists as they climbed onto the dock. "I think we need to know more about the Caribbean life. And I know just the person to ask," she said.

Kimberly had joined her at the window. "Ah, I see where you're going here. Well then, I'll leave you to it. And maybe I can chat with some board members and scare up a bit more on our dear, departed Vanessa."

"Good. We have a plan," Dulcie replied.

Kimberly rubbed her hands together in anticipation, then picked up her purse. "I'll be in touch!" she said scooting out the door.

Dulcie just nodded. Her own thoughts were spinning already.

CB

Adam Johnson hadn't been birding in quite some time. He hoisted the knapsack over his shoulder as he closed the car door behind him and headed down the public walking trail through the woods. He'd cleaned the lenses of his binoculars and pre-adjusted them so that he would only need to make the finer adjustments when needed. In his bag was an identification book, a notebook, pencil, and of course one or two chocolate bars. You never knew when you'd need the extra energy. He slipped the binoculars around his neck and set out.

The path was a bit muddy in places, but he didn't mind. He wasn't there for the exercise, although he knew he needed it. That wasn't the point today. No, today was all about the element of surprise. He'd purposefully chosen to park at the other end of the trail, away from Esmerelda's barn. His plan was to work his way back toward the clearing, toward where he hoped to find her with one of her birds.

He took his time, moving as silently as possible. He was listening as much as looking, and wanted to hear everything. At last he heard what he'd hoped for, the sharp cry of a hawk. He stopped, scanning the sky through the binoculars. He caught a glimpse of it just above the treetops. It dipped down suddenly into the branches and Johnson heard a rustling in the undergrowth. He dropped his binoculars back on his chest and moved toward the commotion.

He sensed Esmerelda's presence before he actually saw her. Funny how that was possible with some people. He stopped when she came into view, picked up his binoculars and watched her through them for several moments. She was speaking to the hawk with a low voice. He couldn't hear what she was saying, but it sounded like an instruction of some kind. He wondered if hawks really could follow instruction but doubted it. Maybe if was just the tone of her voice.

He saw her pick up something from the ground and suddenly throw it at the bird. It squawked as it flapped away from the object at the last second. Johnson was surprised. Was it a rock? Did she intend to hit the bird? She was so protective of her hawks, so why throw something at one deliberately? Was it in anger?

Esmerelda had her own binoculars hanging from her neck as well. She picked them up and looked through them toward the hawk. Then, very slowly, she turned seemingly sweeping through the forest until Johnson realized she was looking directly back at him. He jumped reflexively at having been found out to be spying on her and was instantly annoyed with himself. He dropped the heavy binoculars onto his chest again, gave a half-wave, and quietly moved toward her.

She turned away. He couldn't see her face. But she didn't move. She let him approach. She seemed to be intent on watching the hawk which was, in turn, intent on staring at one spot on the ground. As Johnson drew nearer, Esmerelda put up one hand to stop him, then she moved forward and kicked at the dirt and leaves. The hawk swooped in, grabbed something small and wriggling with its beak, flapped its strong wings, and glided into a nearby tree.

Esmerelda turned back to Johnson. "Why are you spying on me?" she said sharply.

Johnson had had time to think. He knew what to say. "Actually, that wasn't my intent. I saw you with the bird and didn't want to interfere so I watched to see when I could approach."

"Oh," Esmerelda replied simply. Johnson noticed that her shoulders drooped slightly. "But you did see me throw the rock."

"Yes, I did," Johnson answered quietly. "Can I ask why?"

"Yes. I was wondering how Arthur here would react. I'm a good shot, so I wasn't about to hit him, but I did want to get close enough so he'd want to move if he thought it necessary."

"And he did, I saw," Johnson replied.

"Yes, he did," Esmerelda answered.

"What does that tell you?" Johnson asked. It was an innocent enough question.

"It tells me that either Igraine wasn't able to get out of the way quickly enough, or she didn't even see the object coming," Esmerelda said without emotion.

"And what does *that* tell you," Johnson pressed further.

Esmerelda sighed. She looked up at Arthur devouring his latest prey. "It tells me that someone knew what they were doing, and they had a very good arm. Either that or they were very, very lucky."

Johnson nodded. Esmerelda didn't appear to want to move from the spot where they stood until Arthur was done with his meal. Johnson decided to take advantage of the situation. "I understand you were in the Caribbean some time ago? St. John I believe, although perhaps Tortola as well?" he asked the question as innocently as possible.

"You've done your homework," Esmerelda replied. "I'd have expected that. Yes, I was."

"Can I ask what you were doing there?" Johnson said.

There was no use in being evasive Esmerelda realized. She might as well tell him the truth. "I was working with the hawks, of course, training them in surveillance techniques."

Johnson was surprised. "Surveillance? Of what?"

"I'm not exactly sure," Esmerelda said. "It's when I started the work with the video cameras attached to them. I'd answered an ad from someone on St. John who wanted to train some hawks. A private security company. When I got there, they said there was an additional element to the project, the video cameras. I never really knew why the video. I learned quickly that when dealing with security, you don't ask. They hired me to fly the hawks over certain areas at specific times and record the flight. I then had to get the cameras back to them quickly afterward. So I did."

"Weren't you curious as to why they wanted this work done?" Johnson asked.

"Of course, but everything seemed straightforward. I did the job they asked, they paid me in cash, and that was that," Esmerelda replied.

"Were you ever concerned that there was something illegal going on, especially with cash payments?" Johnson asked.

"At first I wasn't," Esmerelda replied. "A lot of people have a lot of reasons for using cash, especially with short-term projects, so I didn't really think about it. Typically, it's just to avoid a small mountain of paperwork. But as time went on, let's just say I became wary. I finally reached a point where I found a way to conclude things and got out of there. That's when I moved to Maine."

"I see," Johnson said. Oddly, he believed her. It explained why she had been fearful when she first reported Igraine's death. Perhaps she thought there had been something illegal going on and these people had sought her out again? He decided not to press the issue just yet.

"I understand you'd met Fiona on Tortola, and that's how she and Rupert wound up here, correct?" Johnson stated.

Esmerelda nodded. "Yes, I was surprised when she contacted me and suggested this project. It was by email, so she thought I was still in the Caribbean. I had to explain I was up here now. I'm not sure she was altogether happy with that, but Rupert seemed thrilled. To be honest," she looked pointedly at Johnson, "I'm happy to have him here. It's a new line of work for my birds, scientific research, and I'd much prefer to be involved with that than with something that was so secretive."

Johnson understood. Esmerelda was a straightforward woman. Her world was black or white. The gray area where most people operated was exceedingly uncomfortable for her.

Yet he also knew that uncomfortable people, frightened people, could do unusual, uncomfortable, frightening things. Once they entered that zone, it was as though their minds couldn't function properly, so they mimicked or even mirrored the behaviors that they were attempting to deal with. It brought about some very odd scenarios.

Esmerelda whistled in a low, long tone to Arthur and held up her arm. He glanced down at her then flapped his wings and flew down to the heavy leather glove on her hand. She quickly grabbed the jess and laced it through her fingers, securing him to her.

Johnson watched the seamless process. This was the world where she was comfortable, with birds. Not with people. She understood her hawks.

Suddenly, Johnson realized that she did, in fact, understand her hawks very well. He remembered what Arthur had done to Rupert. "Esmerelda," Johnson said, "Why do you think Arthur pecked Rupert like that?"

Esmerelda stopped suddenly. Arthur's feathers rose silently, then fell again. The wind had increased and now whistled through the tops of the trees. She stared at the hawk as though trying to see through him. Finally, she said, "I don't know exactly, but it can be only one of two things. Either Arthur felt threatened and needed to establish dominance, or he thought he saw food of some kind and was just trying to get it."

"Hmmm," Johnson said. Esmerelda had begun walking again. "Which do you think it was?" he asked.

"I doubt it was food," she answered.

"So he was threatened. And why would Rupert be threatening to Arthur?" Johnson said.

"Don't know. It was strange, that's for sure. He had no reason to be threatened. Maybe Arthur had Rupert confused with someone else? Or maybe the fact that his hand was bare rather than covered with the glove made a difference? Could have been any number of things."

"I see," Johnson said. They had reached the clearing now where Esmerelda had found the dead Igraine. Where Johnson had found the dead Vanessa. "Esmerelda, is it possible to train a hawk to peck at a particular spot?"

Again, the woman stopped. "You mean, is it possible to train a hawk to peck a person's wrist so that she bleeds to death? Possibly. But as I said, if there's food, maybe on that very spot on the wrist, it's not inconceivable that the beak would drill down while snapping the food up. I'm sure you can imagine."

Johnson could, although he really didn't want to. He just nodded.

Arthur flapped hard against the jess, and Esmerelda held on tighter. "Nearly home old man. Hang on. And no more meals for you today." She turned to Johnson. "I need to get him back into the barn. Let me know when you find out about Igraine." With that dismissal she turned and walked back in the direction of her house.

Johnson realized that she had only asked to be informed about Igraine. Did she have no interest in the fact that a dead woman was found in the same spot on

Esmerelda's very own land? No, of course she didn't. That fact didn't pertain to her. Why should she care?

Johnson glanced around the clearing, then slowly followed the path back through the woods to the dirt parking lot where he'd left his car.

℈

Dulcie stood in the afternoon sunshine at the end of the dock and watched the passengers disembark from Dan's boat. He followed the last of them, two attractive young ladies who appeared very happy to be chatting with the athletic and handsome ship's captain. Their smiles faded as Dulcie approached, presuming, Dulcie supposed, that she was 'the girlfriend'.

"Ah, ladies, here's my sister!" Dan said. Both women immediately grinned again realizing that Dulcie was not, in fact, competition. "I'm afraid we'll have to continue our conversation at another time. Maybe the local watering hole up the street this evening?" Dan gestured toward a nearby bar. Both women nodded enthusiastically and waved as they left.

"I see you haven't lost your touch," Dulcie said.

"Never!" Dan laughed. "C'mon down," he said, gesturing toward the deck. The walked down the gangplank and stepped onto the boat. Dan began coiling a nearby line, and Dulcie instinctively did the same. They had grown up on boats. Tidying a deck was second-nature.

"What brings you down here in the middle of the day, other than a whole lot of sunshine?" Dan asked. "You look like you're mulling over something."

"Yes, I am. It's this latest situation, with the board chair," Dulcie replied.

"The dead board chair," Dan corrected.

"Yes," Dulcie agreed. "But also the dead bird."

Dan stopped for a moment, looked out across the water, then nodded, remembering his conversation with Nick and Dulcie about the murdered bird. "Right. I'm with you now. That's an odd one. So, what's up?"

"Well, I'm wondering about sailing in the Caribbean," Dulcie said. "You've been down there. How hard is it to go back and forth between islands, especially if they're in different countries?"

Dan didn't quite see how this related to the dead bird, or the dead woman for that matter, but he knew Dulcie would get to that eventually. "Depends on the islands," he answered. "Some can be pretty strict, others are more loosey-goosey."

"How about St. John and Tortola?" Dulcie asked.

"They have a ferry, so if you're on that you need to show a passport. If you're on your own boat, you still need a passport and you're supposed to check in with authorities, but I haven't always. I mean, if you anchor and snorkel off the side of the boat for a few hours without going on land, nobody will care much. If marine patrol is bored they might ask you some questions or look at your passport, but it isn't a big deal really."

"Unless, of course, you're doing something nefarious," Dulcie said.

"True, however the nefarious tend to avoid marine patrol," Dan laughed.

"And that's my thought exactly," Dulcie replied.

"So how does this all relate to recent events?" Dan asked. "Or can't you talk about it?"

"I can, only because I'm not even sure how, or if, it relates. We found out that Esmerelda, the one with the dead bird, first became acquainted with Rachel's brother's girlfriend in Tortola. But before that, we only knew that Esmerelda was on St. John."

"Ah, I see," Dan nodded. "You're thinking it might be odd that she's on one island, then the other. Not really, though. It's easy to go back and forth."

Dulcie tied off the line that she'd coiled and put it neatly on the deck. "That's exactly what I needed to know. Now I just wish I could make it fit into the puzzle," she sighed.

"Can't help you with that," Dan said. "But thanks for helping me with the lines. You can be a deck hand any time!"

Dulcie shook her head. "Just protecting the investment," she replied. She was her brother's silent partner, but knew she never had to give the boat a second thought. Dan's easygoing nature suddenly swerved into an obsessive-compulsive bent when it came to boat maintenance.

She walked slowly back along the dock to the brick sidewalk. Commercial Street was busy. It had begun to have the feel of summer when tourists dotted the waterfront. The heat from the sunshine radiated up from the bricks. It felt good on Dulcie's legs after such a long, cold winter.

She imagined being in the Caribbean sun, sailing on turquoise waters. She pictured hawks swooping overhead. No one would pay much attention to them.

Dulcie paused at the door to the museum. She looked up. A seagull flew over. She would never have noticed it if she hadn't actually looked.

Rachel was at her desk as Dulcie went by. She glanced over at her assistant. Rachel looked distracted, almost upset. "Everything ok?" Dulcie asked.

Rachel looked startled, as though she hadn't noticed Dulcie come in. "Yeah, more or less," she said. "I just have this uneasy feeling. I don't like it," she said.

Dulcie nodded. "Yeah, me too," she agreed. She went into her office and shut the door. She didn't like any of this. Rachel was typically confident. She took the initiative, which was why she was so good at her job. Dulcie didn't like this side of her. It seemed uncomfortable, even unnatural. "I need to figure this out," Dulcie whispered to the quiet room. "This has to end."

But how? That was the question she kept asking.

☙

Johnson met Nick on the sidewalk outside Roaster's and opened the door for him. The two went in and Johnson slid into their usual booth as Nick ordered coffee. He joined his partner moments later.

"What have you got?" Nick said.

"It's interesting," Johnson replied, blowing over the top of his mug. "We got the name of the bank used by Rich's Estate Auctions. I've been looking at the accounts. Nothing exciting, just buying and selling stuff. But then I came across some payments to a security company."

"Why would that be unusual?" Nick asked. "They probably handled some valuable antiques, so they'd need to take extra precautions from time to time. Insurance might require it."

"True," Johnson nodded. "Still, I wouldn't be doing due diligence if I didn't look them up, so I did. Just so happens that they're located in the US Virgin Islands."

Nick had just taken his first sip of hot coffee and struggled to swallow. He finally did and set down the mug hard, slopping the liquid over the sides. "What?!" he said.

"You boys all right?" the woman behind the counter called over to them.

Johnson grinned at her. "Yup. Just caught my colleague off guard here!" he said.

She waved at them and turned away, knowing them well enough to ignore their antics.

"You're joking," Nick said, grabbing a paper napkin and wiping up the spill.

"Nope. And furthermore, I checked dates. Payments were made at the same time that Esmerelda was down there. Seems kinda coincidental, don't you think?" Johnson said.

"More than," Nick replied. "Are they the same company that Esmerelda worked for?" he asked.

"I emailed her to get the name of the company. She hasn't replied yet," Johnson pulled out his phone and checked it again. He'd only recently learned how to access email from it, but only used it to read messages. His stubby fingers had difficulty with the tiny keypad, so he didn't dare try to send anything with it.

"Let's assume it is," Nick said. "So Rich Estate Auctions has security activities going on, meanwhile Esmerelda has her hawks flying around doing surveillance for the same company."

"Then Esmerelda leaves abruptly and moves to Maine. Then, Vanessa and her husband move to Maine," Johnson said.

"Then Rupert and Fiona come to Maine, with Fiona having been in contact with at least Esmerelda prior to coming here, but in Tortola and not St. John where Esmerelda had been living," Nick said. He leaned back against the seat. "I think we're getting somewhere," he added.

Johnson leaned back as well and looked up at the ceiling fan. "But where, exactly?" he asked.

They were both silent.

"An estate auction company would be dealing with some pricey antiques, correct?" Johnson said. It was a rhetorical question. "And if those antiques were going from one country to another, wouldn't there be tariffs or something involved?"

"Oddly enough," Nick replied, "In this scenario, no. There are no tariffs on antiques. They have to be over 100 years old, or something like that, to qualify as actual antiques but for some reason, the government doesn't take their cut of them. Don't ask me how I know that. I remember it from law school, I think."

"Wasn't gonna ask," Johnson said. "Don't care how you know. But we're both thinking along the same line, which is smuggling. However, there'd be no reason to smuggle anything if there's not a tax, right?"

Nick was straining his memory, trying to recall what he'd learned in class. There were no tariffs on antiques, but he remembered something else. At last he snapped his fingers. "Use Tax! That's it!"

"How does that fit?" Johnson looked skeptical.

"Most states charge what they call a Use Tax. It's like a Sales Tax."

"What'll they think of next?" Johnson said.

"But for something like this," Nick said, ignoring his partner, "They have to rely on people being honest and reporting items they've bought."

"Which I'm sure is often easily 'overlooked' at tax time," Johnson interjected.

"Correct," Nick said. "However, if there's an official record of the item coming into the country, such as through customs, then the states would have a report of the sale and then they could easily charge the tax."

"So, smuggling in something could save thousands, depending on the value of the item," Johnson concluded.

"Exactly," Nick said. "Exactly," he repeated quietly as he sipped his coffee. Now they were indeed getting somewhere.

❦

It wasn't that Elias couldn't remember. It was that his brain didn't want to. Whenever his thoughts strayed in that direction his mind reflexively shut them down. He knew it was all there, but something in him also knew that he couldn't handle it. It was too disturbing. Better to put it neatly into a box and never allow the box to open.

"Dad?"

The voice crept into his brain slowly. The whistling of the teakettle suddenly became apparent. Elias looked over at it from where he was sitting at the kitchen table. The table where he had found the note that he had steamed open over the same teakettle.

His son walked across the room and slid the kettle away from the burner as he switched it off. "You okay, Dad?" Anderson asked.

Elias looked up at him. He felt as though he was floating, like he was watching a dream of himself in the kitchen with the teakettle. He blinked hard several times, then forced himself to nod.

"I'll make you some tea," Anderson said.

Elias nodded again and waited for his son to put the hot mug in front of him. He wrapped his hands around it. Anderson sat down at the table with his own mug.

"Andy, what if I've done something and I can't remember?" Elias finally said aloud. His voice was soft with a hint of fear.

Anderson inhaled slowly. "Dad, I know what you're thinking, and I don't believe you could have done it."

Elias now shook his head. "You don't know what it was like," he responded. "You don't know what a

209

monster she was." He took a quick sip of the tea. "I locked my bedroom door every night, Andy."

Anderson knew that his parents' relationship had grown distant, but he had no idea it had reached anything close to this level of distrust. "Dad, why didn't you talk to me? Were you afraid of her? Did she threaten you?" He stopped himself from asking more questions even though they were now swirling through his mind.

Tears began to well in Elias's eyes. "Yes, I was afraid. I...," he gulped and took another swallow of hot tea. "I don't know if I was afraid of her or just afraid. She didn't threaten me directly. She just seemed more and more menacing. And secretive. I know she was doing something that she didn't want me to know about. She opened new bank accounts and started moving money around. I asked about it but regretted that instantly – you know how she could get when you asked her a question she didn't want to answer."

Anderson murmured his agreement. He certainly knew. He wished he had known more of this so that he could have helped his father. "Why didn't you tell me?" he asked.

"You had escaped," Elias said simply. "I didn't want to bring you back in. You had begun to make your own life. Your mother had moved her focus on to other things, and that gave you your freedom. The last thing that I wanted to do was to take that away from you."

"So, you suffered alone?" Guilt was now seeping into Anderson's heart. He should have known. And now, what if his father had done something awful?

Could they plead temporary insanity? He forced himself to put that thought aside.

He had another idea. "Dad, I'd like to clean out Mom's office," he said. "I know you don't want to tackle it. I'll sort through her things and get rid of her stuff. Wouldn't that help?" He tried to sound optimistic.

Elias quickly wiped his eyes and drank more tea. "Yes," he whispered. Then he reached over and grabbed his son's wrist, holding it tightly. Anderson slipped his hand into his father's. His palm felt cold in spite of having just been wrapped around the hot mug. Anderson put his other hand around his father's also. "No worries, Dad. No worries," he said. "You're safe. I've got this. You raised me to be a good man, and I'm going to help you."

Tears now rolled down Elias's face. Words croaked in his throat, but he couldn't get them out. Anderson was now out of his chair, hugging his father tightly, rocking him back and forth. "It's over, Dad. It's over. No worries. I'll make sure everything is okay."

Anderson wasn't sure how long he stayed with his father, reassuring him. His sobbing had been uncontrollable at first, the release from years of mounting unhappiness, fear, loneliness. When Anderson felt him begin to relax, he suggested that he lie down and rest.

Elias agreed. He felt exhausted. Drained. He allowed his son to walk him into his bedroom. Anderson pulled a heavy quilt over him, drew the curtains, and quietly closed the door.

He went directly to his mother's office. "Damn bitch," he said aloud. It was the first time he'd dared say something like that. He had never even dared think it before even though he'd come close many times. He knew she was mean, overbearing, a bully at heart. He should have been doing more to help his father though.

Anderson yanked out all of the drawers from his mother's desk and lined them up on a side table. He shoved open the roll top, nearly breaking it in the process. He was going to get to the bottom of all of this. She was gone now. Dead. Anderson had done nothing to help his father while she was alive, but he'd do whatever it took to make sure she didn't reach out from the grave and ruin his dad's life now.

ಐ

Fiona woke with a start. The room was dark. She'd decided to lie down after talking with the police earlier. It had drained her. Evidently, she'd fallen asleep. Now she rolled her head over to the side and glanced at the clock beside the bed. Seven-thirty. Her stomach growled.

Fiona shifted her head on the pillow again and realized that the bedroom door was open. The whole apartment was dark. Rupert was probably downstairs in the barn.

She was about to get up when she heard the door open at the foot of the stairs. That would be Rupert. She heard footsteps easing up the stairs. Nice of him to be quiet since she'd been sleeping, Fiona thought. She was about to call out to him when she heard it – the loud squeak from the fourth step.

Fiona's heart began to pound. Rupert knew about that step. He avoided it more than she did, annoyed by the sound. This wasn't Rupert.

The footsteps paused, then continued slowly, quietly. Fiona shifted her weight off the bed as silently as possible. She picked up the first large, heavy object she could find – one of Rupert's work boots. It wasn't perfect, but it would have to do. Tiptoeing in stocking feet, she crept to the doorway and saw a shadow moving across the front room toward the desk. The person picked up something.

Fiona stepped forward, about to hit them with the boot, but tripped on the carpet. She stumbled, and the person turned quickly. "Who are you?" Fiona managed to say before she felt something hard hit her. The person shoved her back into the bedroom, and she fell with a thud on the floor. Fiona heard loud stomping down the stairs, then heavy footsteps running outside, into the woods.

Fiona stood as quickly as she could and looked out the window. Everything seemed calm. It was as though none of it had happened. Had it happened? Did she just imagine someone in her home? Was this just a bad dream and she was about to wake up?

She looked down the stairs half expecting someone to appear. The door was open below. Turning on a light, she now sat on the top step and stared down onto the worn barn floor below. She could hear the birds chirping.

This was not a dream, but it felt like the nightmare that had become her life was increasingly real. Whatever they had hit her with had landed squarely against her upper arm. She rubbed it now. There would be a bruise soon.

She hated this place. She had to get out. When she felt as though she could stand, she slowly made her way downstairs, carefully avoiding the fourth step.

The birds were still chirping softly. Strange that they hadn't called out when the intruder had gone by. Fiona thought for a moment. What if it hadn't been an intruder? What if the birds had known who it was?

Fiona began to shake. That left only two options: Rupert and Esmerelda. Rupert wasn't an option – he knew she was there, plus he knew about the squeak in the step. No, it had to be Esmerelda.

At that moment Fiona heard a sound from the other side of the barn. She turned quickly, terrified that it was Esmerelda.

Rupert had just stepped through the open door. "Oh, thank god it's you!" Fiona said and raced toward him.

He caught her as she nearly fell into his arms. "What? What is it?" he said. "Fifi, you're shaking!"

She was nearly hysterical now with fear. "Someone was upstairs," she said. "I think it was Esmerelda. She stole something! And she tried to hurt me!"

Rupert held her tightly. "Are you sure?" he said. "Did you see her? What was stolen?"

They went upstairs as Fiona tried to calm herself and relate everything that had happened. Her heart was still pounding. She sat on the couch while Rupert looked around the room. Within moments he realized what was missing.

"They took the laptop," he said.

"Your research?" Fiona said. "Now what?"

Rupert sat down beside her. "No, don't worry about that. I have a backup. Besides, the most important thing is that you weren't hurt," he said.

"No," she said, her voice shaking. "Just my arm where she hit me."

"She hit you?!" Rupert exclaimed.

"With the laptop, I think," Fiona said, rubbing her arm. "She was shoving me away, trying to get by."

Fiona leaned against Rupert and he put his arm around her, thinking about what to do next. They should call the police, certainly.

CB

Nick had just finished dinner with Dulcie at her townhouse when his cell phone rang. "Johnson?" Nick answered, knowing it was his partner. "Yep. Be right there. Fill me in on the way," he said.

Dulcie was carrying dishes back into the kitchen. She stopped and turned back toward him. "Lemme guess, I'm on cleanup duty alone," she said.

"Yeah, 'fraid so," Nick said. "Sorry!" he already had his jacket half on and swooped in for a quick kiss. "I'll call you as soon as I can," he added.

"Just tell me one thing. Is this about Vanessa?" she asked.

"What do you think?" Nick replied. He didn't wait for an answer as he closed the door behind him.

The night was quiet. An onshore breeze gently moved across the chilly Atlantic, cooling the air. Nick pulled the zipper of his jacket halfway up and slid behind the wheel of the car. Moments later he pulled over in front of the police station and Johnson got in.

"What do you have?" Nick asked.

"Enough," Johnson replied. "Vanessa's son was sorting through her desk, getting things in order. He came across emails between her and Esmerelda."

"Really!" Nick exclaimed.

"Seems we were right. They were in touch in the Caribbean. Esmerelda found out enough about what was happening with Vanessa's smuggling down there and pulled out. Vanessa was furious. She followed her to Maine and threatened her with exposure for her part in the scheme. My guess is that Esmerelda arranged to meet Vanessa that morning, had trained the bird well enough to at least scare off Vanessa, and maybe got lucky that Vanessa died," Johnson said.

"Or maybe didn't get lucky since it's murder," Nick replied. "But what about this robbery that just happened?"

"Fiona was in her apartment this evening and someone stole their laptop while she was there," Johnson said.

"Rupert and Fiona's laptop? Why take that?" Nick asked. "Oh wait, was it the videos? Maybe there are others like the one with Vanessa?"

"Possibly," Johnson answered. "Fiona said that she heard Esmerelda run into the woods."

"She ran into the woods?" Nick said. "How do we know that was Esmerelda then?"

"Because the fourth step squeaked and the birds didn't," Johnson replied.

Nick said nothing but glanced over at his partner.

"Watch the road, please," Johnson admonished. "I'll explain."

"Please do!" Nick said.

"Fiona thinks that the intruder didn't know she was there. She'd fallen asleep and the place was dark. The person coming up the steps walked on the fourth step which always has a hideous squeak. She and Rupert avoid it. Also, when the person ran out, the birds didn't call out so they must have known the intruder. They squawk when someone they don't know is there but they're usually pretty quiet when it's someone they do know," Johnson clarified.

"Ah, now I get it. But do we have enough to arrest her?" Nick was thinking out loud.

"Enough to bring her in on suspicion anyway," Johnson said.

"We'll need to locate the laptop though," Nick added. He steered the car into the long driveway and pulled up next to the barn, blocking the entrance. The outdoor light came on and the door slid open. Fiona and Rupert appeared.

Nick and Johnson got out of the car. "Where is she?" Johnson asked. Rupert pointed over toward the house. "Stay in there, please," Nick said to the couple, jerking his head toward the barn.

The two men went to the small house on the property and knocked on the door. Rupert and Fiona peeked outside. They saw the door open and watched as words were exchanged. Esmerelda looked angry. They saw her step back inside, then she came out with a jacket. Johnson and Nick escorted her back to the police car. The three of them got in and unceremoniously left.

Rupert and Fiona looked at each other. "Well that was odd!" Rupert said.

"Do you think she actually did it?" Fiona asked.

"She must have," Rupert replied.

"But why did she want our laptop?" Fiona wondered.

"Maybe for the video? I've seen people out on the trails, so maybe she thought there would be video of her out there? Or the dead woman?" Rupert replied.

"Yes, that makes sense," Fiona said. It didn't make her feel any better though. "Rupert, we can leave here now, right? I mean, a woman is dead, I've been attacked, and even though the police have Esmerelda now, I still feel like I need to get as far away as we can. I don't like this place. Please, can we leave?" Tears welled in her eyes as she pleaded with him.

Rupert put his arms around her and held her close. "Yes, Fifi, I think that's a very good idea, given the circumstances," he said. "A very good idea, indeed."

*I think that if you shake the tree,
you ought to be around
when the fruit falls
to pick it up.*
~ Mary Cassatt

CHAPTER THIRTEEN

"I'm going out for lunch today," Rachel told Dulcie as she handed her a mug of coffee.

"Really?" Dulcie replied. Rachel nearly always ate at her desk, preferring to 'keep an eye on things' as she put it. "Is this a hot date?" Dulcie asked slyly.

"Hardly," Rachel said. "I'm meeting Rupert and Fiona. They're leaving on the red-eye tonight from Boston."

"Leaving? As in, packing their bags and leaving for good?" Dulcie was surprised. "Isn't this a little sudden?"

Rachel nodded. "Fiona is spooked by everything that happened. You know the weird hawk lady got arrested, right?"

Dulcie did indeed know. Nick had told her the night before once he and Johnson had brought Esmerelda to the police station. "Yes, I knew that of course," Dulcie replied, sipping her coffee.

"Did you know that Fiona got hurt when Esmerelda broke in to the apartment?"

"What?" Dulcie exclaimed. She'd only had a brief phone conversation with Nick. He hadn't had time for details.

"Oooh, I know something you don't know!" Rachel said gleefully.

"Yes, you do," Dulcie replied. "So, spill it."

"Rachel took a long drink of her coffee and set down the mug carefully to prolong the moment. Dulcie rolled her eyes. "Okay," Rachel began, "Evidently, Esmerelda broke in to their apartment over the barn while Fiona was there and stole their laptop."

"How can she break in when it's her apartment?" Dulcie quipped.

"Not relevant," Rachel countered. "Fiona had decided to lie down later in the afternoon and fell asleep. She woke up after the sun had gone down so the place was dark. She heard someone come in and realized it wasn't Rupert. I guess Esmerelda thought no one was home. She'd already grabbed the laptop when Fiona surprised her. Esmerelda hit her with the computer, and shoved her out of the way, then ran downstairs and out into the woods."

"Wait," Dulcie said putting up her hand. "How did she know it was Esmerelda?"

"She didn't. They didn't find that out until later." Rachel replied.

Now Dulcie was really confused. "And why did she want the laptop?"

Rachel shrugged her shoulders. "Don't know," she said.

Dulcie's brain was spinning. "And isn't Rupert very concerned, not just for Fiona but also about his research? Wasn't he borderline obsessive about it?"

Rachel now stood. Mentally she had already moved on to her next task. "He definitely is obsessive, but he does backups religiously, so he's not worried about that."

Dulcie began to ask another question, but Rachel stopped her. "You know what I know now. Gotta go. Things to do!" she said. She sauntered out of the room.

Dulcie put her elbows on the ugly laminate surface of the table as she sipped her coffee. The old Rachel was back, and Dulcie was glad of it. Yet something wasn't adding up with the whole case. It was as though the pieces of the puzzle had been forced together, but they didn't quite form the image that they should. Dulcie let her mind wander for a few more moments, but then shook her head vigorously. No, she had work to do as well. She'd best get on with it.

"Where's your trusty sidekick?"

Dulcie looked up with surprise to see Nick standing in the doorway. She glanced at her watch. It was lunchtime. "Oh, she went to lunch with her brother and his girlfriend. Seems they're heading out tonight."

Nick crossed the room and sat down. He reached under the table and squeezed Dulcie's knee. She grinned at him. "That's the only advantage to having this horrid table rather than my old desk," she said. "Oh, and Rachel filled me in on events that transpired with Fiona."

Nick exhaled a long, low breath.

"It isn't adding up, is it," Dulcie said.

One of the many things that Nick loved about Dulcie was her ability to size up a situation very quickly, and in very few words. "No," he replied. "No, it isn't."

"What does Esmerelda have to say?" Dulcie asked.

"She maintains her innocence. She admitted to knowing Vanessa, and she'd already talked to Johnson a little about working with the hawks in the Caribbean on a surveillance project, but I just don't see the motivation to kill Vanessa. Esmerelda says Vanessa was threatening her, saying she'd reveal Esmerelda's work with the hawks as illegal surveillance. She was also demanding money. But if Esmerelda did nothing wrong, or even if she did but wasn't aware of it at the time, why not just report Vanessa's blackmail attempts to the police?"

"And why go to all the trouble to use a hawk to kill her?" Dulcie added. "Seems like a lot of work to get a hawk to do that. Unless it truly was an accident of some kind. Like the murdered hawk. Maybe that was an accident too?"

The murdered hawk. Nick stared at the fake wood surface on the table. The lines squiggled and undulated to form patterns that, at first glance looked like wood grain but, on closer inspection, were just lines that someone had drawn. It was all an illusion. He looked back up at Dulcie.

"You've got it, haven't you," she said.

"I think so," Nick replied.

"What next?" Dulcie asked.

"Can you meet me at Esmerelda's barn in a couple of hours?" Nick was out of his seat and dialing his cell phone.

"Of course!" Dulcie replied to his back. He was already out the door.

ɣ

At three o'clock, Dulcie stood in Esmerelda's shadowy barn listening to the hawks calling out softly. She'd arrived several minutes before and her eyes had grown accustomed to the low light. She heard a car drive up outside and wasn't surprised to see Elias Rich and his son Anderson emerge. They blinked when they came into the barn, seeing only darkness at first, just as Dulcie had done. She didn't say anything, just waited for them to notice her.

Another car pulled in. Johnson got out and opened the door to the back seat. Esmerelda stepped out. She glanced into the barn warily. Her eyes pierced through the darkness. 'Like a hawk, of course,' Dulcie thought.

A noise behind Dulcie made her turn. She saw Nick coming down the stairs followed by Rupert and Fiona. Dulcie was surprised to see Rachel too. As they reached the bottom, Fiona stopped suddenly. Esmerelda had just come in.

"What's she doing here?" Fiona shrieked, pointing at Esmerelda. "She's supposed to be in jail! She attacked me! Get her out of here!"

Johnson stepped forward. "Calm down," he said quietly. Esmerelda remained silent.

Nick moved over to the heavy sliding door and shoved it open as much as possible, letting in more light. He turned and faced the others. He was well aware that with the bright light behind him, they could only see his silhouette.

"This all began with a dead bird," he said calmly. He watched everyone carefully. Brows furrowed.

"Not just any dead bird," Nick continued, "But a highly trained hawk, obviously killed and left in a clearing. Why would someone do that?"

They were all silent for a moment. Finally, Anderson spoke up. "To leave a message?" he said.

"To leave a message," Nick repeated. "Correct. And for Esmerelda, the message was received loud and clear." Nick walked back into the barn and stood beside her. "Isn't that right, Esmerelda? That's why you came to us. That's why you reported Igraine as 'murdered.' Because she had been. But you couldn't tell us the whole story, could you."

Esmerelda shook her head. Her face was expressionless.

"And that's because you were afraid. And you were hoping we would find out on our own, correct?"

This time Esmerelda nodded.

"Which it seems we have," Nick said softly. "Let's step back in time a bit. As most of you know, Esmerelda lived on St. John in the U.S. Virgin Islands for a while, working with her birds. While there, she was hired to do various projects. She also met you there," Nick pointed to Fiona, "Leading to your presence here."

"Something that I regret deeply," Fiona said, her voice shaking.

"I'm sure," Nick replied. He turned back to Esmerelda. "You also met someone else in the Caribbean although you weren't immediately aware of it, were you."

Esmerelda shook her head. It seemed that she couldn't speak, or she had been instructed not to.

"You were hired to use your hawks for surveillance," Nick continued. "Specifically, surveillance between St. John and the neighboring island of Tortola, which happens to be part of the British Virgin Islands." Nick glanced around the group. Brows were still furrowed. He wasn't surprised. It was a complicated story.

"It probably wasn't long before you realized that the work that you were doing was not exactly legal. At that point, you extricated yourself as soon as you could and relocated far away. But it wasn't far enough."

Esmerelda looked at the heavy wooden planks on the floor now. Her shoulders began to sag.

"You established yourself here in Maine. During that time, you were contacted by Rupert, by way of Fiona, to ask about using the hawks for research work. You jumped at the chance. This would establish you in a new line of business that was certainly much safer than

225

surveillance. In the meantime though, someone else appeared. Someone else had decided to move to Maine and you knew exactly why. It was the same person who had hired you in the Virgin Islands, correct?"

Again, Esmerelda nodded.

"That person was Vanessa Rich," Nick announced. He paused for a moment. "I don't think I'll be offending anyone, although I apologize if I am, if I speak ill of her, but Vanessa had a way of making enemies."

Rachel snorted quietly as she stood beside Dulcie. Dulcie elbowed her.

"Vanessa had the ability to find people's weaknesses quickly, and had no problem with exploiting them. She was able to gain positions of influence and wielded her power to throw everyone off balance. She had used her husband's skills in finance to set up a business selling antiques. She then wormed her way on the museum board and began selling off items there where she would make a hefty commission, starting with Dulcie's office furniture. That had the added bonus of showing Dulcie that she, Vanessa, was the one in charge. She was able to control everyone around her by either throwing them off balance with her constant maneuvers, knowing secrets about them that they wouldn't want revealed, or setting them up in situations that she could then use against them."

Nick stopped, hearing a groan from the side of the room. Elias had reached out to hold onto a heavy support beam, his knees shaking. Anderson put his arm round him, holding him up as Johnson scurried into the office to get a chair. He ran back out with it as Anderson lowered his father onto the seat.

Nick realized he needed to speed this up. At that moment, they heard another car outside. A door opened and closed, then Nick saw Kimberly come through the door, blinking in the comparative darkness. Dulcie quickly moved over to her and whispered something. Kimberly moved to stand by Elias Rich, watching him intently. Dulcie now whispered to Anderson, "She knows your father, and she's a nurse." Anderson nodded, looking relieved.

Nick was relieved as well. "I'll continue," he said. "So, at this point, everyone is now here in Maine. Esmerelda finds her bird dead, obviously killed. She knows Vanessa must have done it as a warning. Esmerelda then tries to frighten off Vanessa but it goes horribly wrong, and Vanessa winds up dead."

"Case closed," said Rupert. "Except why steal my laptop?"

"Why indeed?" Nick agreed. "Because you had video recordings from the birds that would link Vanessa and Esmerelda. Or so we were made to believe."

Everyone looked at Nick curiously.

"You see," Nick said, "Looking at this one way, this seemed to be an open and shut case. Vanessa tricked Esmerelda into doing illegal work, then threatened to expose her secret unless she paid up. Esmerelda killed Vanessa. End of story. But that's not how it really happened," Nick added. "Is it, Rupert."

The entire group gasped at once.

"What?!" Rupert exclaimed. "What are you talking about?"

Esmerelda was now staring at him intently. She couldn't hold back any longer. "You killed her!" she exclaimed. Dulcie wasn't sure if Esmerelda meant Vanessa or Igraine, but judging by her level of anger, she assumed it was the latter. Esmerelda probably cared more about the fate of her birds than any human.

Rupert had turned pale.

"She's right," Nick said quietly. "You learned quickly what had happened between Esmerelda and Vanessa, and saw a golden opportunity. You had recordings of them in the woods. You killed the bird, knowing that Esmerelda would believe that Vanessa had done it as a warning. Then you began posing as Esmerelda using emails, and blackmailed Vanessa about her illegal smuggling of antiques from Tortuga to St. John. You even threw in the anonymous note, hoping Elias would see it which would ratchet up the stakes for Vanessa. But the problem was, Vanessa played the game better than you and she found out that it was you, not Esmerelda, blackmailing her. However, Vanessa didn't know that *you* knew she was on to you. That's when you realized Vanessa had to go, and you had to pin the blame on Esmerelda."

Gasps and murmurers were now floating around the barn. Fiona had slowly begun to step away from Rupert.

"You set up a ruse for Vanessa to meet Esmerelda in the clearing on the morning when Esmerelda was leaving early to visit a colleague. You watched Esmerelda leave. Then you went out to the clearing where Vanessa was waiting. She was probably surprised to see you. You must have tripped her or knocked her over first in a way that made it look like she fell. There was evidence that her head was hit, but forensics assumed it was from a fall." Nick stopped, thinking of how he would word the next part. With Elias already unwell, he didn't want to be graphic with the explanation.

"Your next move was the brilliant bit. She was attacked by a hawk, and that's what killed her. A hawk had sunk its beak into the exact spot on her wrist that would ensure she would quickly die from loss of blood, especially since she was already unconscious."

Now Rupert was shaking. "This is preposterous! How could I get a hawk to do that?" he yelled.

"Easy," said Nick. "The hawk was already dead."

Johnson now stepped forward with a plastic bag. He handed it to Nick, who slowly pulled out the frozen body of Igraine.

"You got the idea from being pecked yourself, didn't you," Nick said. "When Arthur pecked your hand, it was a single wound, but it was deep and decisive. You lost consciousness yourself from it even though you probably wouldn't have lost your life. The wound wasn't in the right place for that. But it was enough to give you the idea and the perfect way to set up Esmerelda. She would be blamed for the murder, and you would have the money you blackmailed. Plus, you would also have all of your research so you could write your dissertation back in England and continue on with your life."

"I'm not listening to any of this!" Rupert shouted. "Besides, she stole my laptop!" he said, pointing at Esmerelda.

"Nope, that was you again," Nick said.

"What?!" Fiona's voice was now a hoarse whisper. "That wasn't Esmerelda?" She turned, backing away further from Rupert. "You shoved me? You hit me?"

Johnson had silently moved behind Rupert. He grabbed both of his wrists and began putting handcuffs on him. Rupert tried to struggle but then gave up. He looked at Fiona. "I had to make it look like a robbery," he said. "I was supposed to bring it to the police when I reported the stupid note, but I couldn't have them going through everything, could I? They'd have found the emails! If you'd just have shut up, we'd have been fine!" He was screaming at her now.

Fiona lunged forward and swung both arms at his chest. Johnson pulled Rupert away, marching him out of the barn as he read him his rights. Fiona sat down heavily on the floor and began sobbing, rocking back and forth.

It was as though all of the oxygen had been sucked out of the large room. The birds had begun shrieking when they heard the shouting, but were now oddly silent. Nick heard Johnson putting Rupert into the car. He knew uniformed officers were waiting there as well.

Elias pulled out a handkerchief and mopped his brow. "I'll get you some water," Kimberly said. "Or something stronger," she added in a whisper to Dulcie as she walked by her.

Rachel looked over at Dulcie, then at Nick. "But," she began, her eyes wide, "But..., why did I get fired?"

"Good question," Nick said. "At first it just seemed like spite. Vanessa needed to show Dulcie who was boss. But then we made the connection between Vanessa and Esmerelda. When Vanessa saw Rupert in the museum and learned that he was your brother, she couldn't let him recognize her. Vanessa had already seen him in the woods near Esmerelda's barn. She couldn't risk him knowing who she was, so she couldn't have him around the museum. The only way to ensure that was to get rid of you, Rachel."

"So, it wasn't me really, it was just my connection to Rupert," Rachel said. "But Vanessa didn't know that Rupert already knew about her and Esmerelda?"

"Correct," Nick said.

"Wow!" Rachel exclaimed. She went over to Fiona, knelt beside her and put an arm around her. "Looks like we both got duped," she said. She turned to Nick. "Are you done with us? Can Fiona and I go talk up there?" She gestured upstairs toward the apartment.

"Yes, go ahead," Nick said. "I think you can go as well," Nick added to Anderson and his father.

Kimberly had been talking with Elias quietly. She wrote something on a card and handed it to Anderson. "Call them," Dulcie heard Kimberly say. "They'll help him through."

... and then, I have nature and art and poetry,
and if that is not enough, what is enough?
~ Vincent van Gogh

CHAPTER FOURTEEN

Dulcie leaned back against the rail of the boat and closed her eyes. The bright sun was warm and the breeze gentle as they putted along slowly. Her hair was pulled back into a glossy ponytail. She felt soft fingers slip one of the tendrils that had strayed loose behind her ear. Dulcie opened her eyes.

A glass of champagne appeared in front of her. "Figured we deserved this," Nick said. He held the glass in one hand and a bottle of her favorite Veuve Clicquot in the other. She reached out with both hands taking the glass and the bottle. Nick laughed. He stepped away, getting his own glass, then joined her again, sitting beside her. Dulcie filled his glass and clinked hers against it.

"Here's to another case successfully in the books," she said.

"I'll drink to that," Nick replied. He savored a large mouthful of the bubbles. "And this wasn't an easy one," he added.

"Are they ever?" Dulcie asked.

"Not really," Nick said. He looked up at the bridge where Dan was lazily steering the boat. Rachel was sitting beside him, drinking a bottle of beer and chatting. "Do you think she's come through all of this all right?" Nick asked.

Dulcie glanced up at Rachel. "Yeah, I think so. We've had a couple of long talks. She didn't grow up with Rupert, really. They were together for a few weeks each year she said, but she felt like he was more of a cousin than a brother. Or *half*-brother, as she now keeps stressing. She said that he was always very affable but secretive too. Even though they got along well, she didn't feel like she ever really knew him."

Nick nodded. "I know the type. Someone who you can have entire conversations with, but you walk away and realize you know nothing about the person."

"Exactly," Dulcie replied. "I think Rachel's happy to have things go back to relative normalcy again. And I must say, so am I."

They watched a seagull swoop across the bow, perhaps looking for a stray scrap left by a careless tourist. "Nice of Dan to give up a tour and let us come out today," Nick said.

"He's good like that," Dulcie agreed. "Plus, I bought the boat, so he kind of has to indulge me from time to time."

Nick laughed. He'd forgotten the arrangement that Dulcie and Dan had made with her inheritance. It was nice to see a brother and sister get along well, especially since his own family experience was less than happy. He thought about Anderson and his father. "Do you think Elias will be okay?"

Dulcie sipped her champagne thoughtfully. She examined the bubbles slowly rising through the amber liquid. "Yes, I think so. Kimberly said he'd decided to sell the house here and move south. Maybe Charleston, she said. Anderson is being very supportive of course, and said he'd find a job near wherever his father wants to be."

"That's good to know," Dan said.

"I agree. Kimberly said that she thinks Anderson feels a little guilty. He feels as though he abandoned his father to deal with his mother alone," Dulcie added.

"I don't know about that," said Nick. "Elias is a grown man. He married Vanessa and chose to stay with her. At some point, people have to face up to their own demons."

"Very true," Dulcie agreed. "I'm just glad that my most recent one is no longer with us," she said. "I'm not allowed to be happy that she's dead. That would be wrong. But I am glad I don't have to deal with her anymore. She was so good at making people miserable." Dulcie sighed.

"It's behind you now," Nick reminded her. "So, what's the next project?" he asked. Best to start moving forward again.

Dulcie laughed. "That was a less than subtle way to change the subject, but I'll go with it!" she said. "Next for me is to find a new desk. I don't want to sound like a diva, but I can't bear that table any longer!"

"You are totally a diva," Nick grinned.

Dulcie smacked him on the arm, nearly sloshing her champagne. "Really though, I do need something with drawers and a surface that doesn't literally bounce when I press on it too hard. And I'm sorry, I know you deal with metal file cabinets at the station, but I can't handle that one any longer." She stuck one leg out in front of her. "Look at the bruises I have from that stupid thing!"

Nick couldn't help himself. He reached out and slid his hand from her ankle all the way up to her knee.

"Hey, hands off my sister!"

Dulcie and Nick looked up quickly to see Dan shouting at them. Rachel was laughing. Nick held his hands up in the air as if in surrender, one still clutching the champagne glass. Dan grinned.

ɤ

Dulcie sipped her morning coffee while sitting at her ugly table in her office. She listening to rain patter softly against the windowsill. The forecast called for brief showers, but the rest of the day would be sunny. Dulcie paged through an online auction catalog of furniture, looking at desks. The board had unanimously approved the purchase of a new one, but Dulcie didn't want to spend a lot. She had convinced herself that all she needed was something functional. And maybe a little bit decorative, too.

She looked up, hearing a commotion just outside her office doorway. Rachel poked her head in. "Delivery for Dr. Chambers!" she announced.

Rachel disappeared, and Dulcie stood, wondering what was happening. She had barely stepped away from the table when an enormous object began emerging from the hallway through the door.

"What...?" Dulcie began.

A carved chestnut desk was slowly being rolled into her office. Rachel stood behind it smiling mischievously. "This came with it," she said as she slid an envelope across the warm, dark surface. It had Dulcie's name written on it.

Dulcie opened the envelope and pulled out the card inside.

Dear Dr. Chambers,

Please accept this gift that I offer to you and the museum. I want you to know that wandering the galleries and attending the lectures at the Maine Museum of Art gave me great pleasure and helped me to endure a very difficult time. As you must know, art has the power to do do many things. Healing is one of them. I am forever grateful for that.

I hope to visit your museum again someday if I am ever back in Maine.

Until then, I remain...

Your friend,
Elias Rich

Speechless, Dulcie looked up at Rachel. "Just put it over here, please," Rachel said. "Where the table is. You can move that into the storage room." The furniture was quickly maneuvered around, and the maintenance crew left, closing the door behind them.

Dulcie hadn't uttered a word. Rachel gestured toward Dulcie's chair. "You might need a new one to match the desk now," she said. "That's looking a little shabby in comparison."

Dulcie sat down in the chair. She looked up at her assistant. "Did you know about this?" she asked.

Rachel nodded vigorously. "Yeah. I mean, not specifically what it looked like, but I figured Elias has good taste, so he'd pick out something nice. I think Kimberly might have had a say, too."

"Kimberly?" Dulcie said. "She was in on this?"

Rachel giggled. "Of course. Who else?"

'Who else, indeed,' Dulcie thought. She ran her hands over the smooth surface of the desk. The hard wood felt almost soft. She'd need to get a blotter so that she wouldn't make dents in it when she wrote with a pen.

"Okay then, I'll just leave you to revel in your new surroundings," Rachel quipped.

Dulcie barely heard her. She was already pulling open the drawers and filling them with the contents of the ugly file cabinets. As she finished, a ray of sunshine spilled through the window and lit up the rich carvings along the edges. Dulcie felt its warmth on her. Yes, things seemed to be looking up.

ଓ

Adam Johnson stepped as lightly as his large framed allowed through the wet underbrush. The sun was now out as the sky cleared. He stopped, listening, and pulled his binoculars up to his eyes.

A hawk perched in a nearby tree, yellow eyes gleaming intently. Johnson saw the leather jess attached to its leg. One of Esmerelda's birds. She must be nearby. He scanned lower, into the bushes beneath and spotted her.

Johnson waited for her to move before he did. She walked slowly in his direction, whistling in a long, low note to the bird as she did. Johnson moved slowly as well. At last they met at the foot of the tree, beneath the bird.

"Not surprised to see you out," Esmerelda said. "Can't stop a chronic birder," she added. It was the closest Johnson had heard her come to saying anything even remotely humorous.

He smiled in acknowledgment. "Nope. That's a fact," he said. It was the first time he'd spoken with her since her release from custody. He cleared his throat. "I should apologize for the mistake...," he began.

Esmerelda waived her hand, stopping him. "No apology needed," she said. "All in the line of work, I know. Just wish I had the same insight into people that I have for birds," she said.

Johnson looked up at the hawk in the tree and recognized him as Arthur. "I've been told my insight into people is very good, which it must be since I've been doing my job for so many years. Yet I'm still fooled, over and over again." He looked back down at Esmerelda. "I'd stick with the hawks," he added.

Esmerelda raised her arm and whistled to Arthur. She held a piece of meat on her gloved hand. Arthur flapped his wings once and swooped down, perching on her leather covered wrist as he deftly grabbed the meat with his sharp beak.

For the first time, Johnson saw Esmerelda smile. It was actually a very nice smile. Johnson wondered how many times she had smiled with her birds. And perhaps how few, if ever, she had smiled with people.

She glanced up at him. "Yes, I'll stick with the hawks," she agreed. "They're a lot less trouble." With that, she turned and disappeared into the woods.

The Dulcie Chambers Mysteries

Book #1
An Exhibit of Madness
(Previously titled: *Portrait of a Murder*)

Dr. Dulcinea ("Dulcie") Chambers has a lot on her mind. She's just opened a new exhibit of Winslow Homer watercolors at the Maine Museum of Art where she's Chief Curator. The exhibit will be complete when the museum's director, the urbane Joshua Harriman, buys the final piece at auction. But when Dulcie discovers a body where the painting should have been, she's one of the primary suspects. Portland Police Detective Nicholas Black is on the case but finds he is less than objective when it comes to the attractive Dr. Chambers.

Book #2
From the Murky Deep

Detective Nicholas Black has cause for concern. He's investigating the suspicious death of a young woman whose body has just washed on shore in full scuba gear. Normally it would simply be a case of drowning, yet along with this particular body is a stolen Vincent van Gogh painting in a watertight tube. To further complicate matters, the phone number of Dr. Dulcinea (Dulcie) Chambers is written on the dead woman's hand. As the new director of the Maine Museum of Art, Dulcie is already busy negotiating the sale of one of the museum's pieces with a wealthy collector. When Dulcie learns that she's a chief suspect however, she has no choice but to help with the investigation. Dulcie finds herself diving in to solve this mystery as her relationship with Detective Nicholas Black also reaches new depths.

Book #3
The Fragile Flower

World-renowned abstract expressionist painter Logan Dumbarton is welcomed to the Maine Museum of Art to teach a master class to a group of talented local artists. But he proves more difficult than any of the staff, along with his stunning yet whiny wife and his spinster/business-manager sister, can handle with his constant complaints and egocentric demeanor. Within a week the entire class loathes him. Is he really worth all this trouble? Somebody doesn't seem to think so and it's up to Dr. Dulcinea ("Dulcie") Chambers to find out who. But she'll have to team up with Detective Nicholas Black once again, and their relationship at the moment can only be described as *fragile*.

Book #4
A Mind Within

While assembling a new exhibit featuring *Art Brut* or "Outsider Art," Dr. Dulcinea ("Dulcie") Chambers encounters an enormously talented and equally troubled young man, Xander Bellamy. An autistic savant, Xander has not communicated with anyone for several months, since his father was sent to prison for the murder of Xander's domineering grandfather. Detective Nicholas

Black thought the case was closed until Dulcie came to him with compelling evidence that the real killer was still at large. When evidence had originally pointed to Xander as the murderer, Xander's father had quickly confessed. Did he do this to save his son from being committed to a mental institution for the criminally insane? Xander's battle-axe aunt has come to live with him and, along with long-time family housekeeper Giselle, they see to his needs. But is there more to them than meets the eye? Meanwhile Dulcie seeks to see inside Xander's mind with the help of psychologist Dr. Raymond Armand. However, the ambitious Armand has other ideas about the lovely Dr. Chambers and is about to give Nicholas Black some competition when it comes to her affections.

Book #5
Last of the Vintage

Dr. Dulcinea Chambers' old boyfriend, the adventurous, fun-loving, and decidedly good-looking Brendan MacArthur, reappears with a unique gift for the Maine Museum of Art: a very old bottle of wine, one of several that he found in a shipwreck while scuba diving in Maine's cold Atlantic waters. With museum attendance low during a particularly brutal winter, Dulcie knows exactly what to do. The museum will host a wine tasting as a fundraiser featuring this old vintage. But when an icebreaker busts through the pack ice in Portland harbor the day after the festivities, the crew makes a gruesome discovery. Someone from the party didn't make it home, and instead wound up among the bobbing gray-blue sheets of ice floating from one side of the harbor to the other.

Dulcie's knowledge of wine is needed by detective Nicholas Black as he sorts through the details of this case, but their budding relationship is also put to the test. Brendan MacArthur's sudden reappearance irritates Nick. Does he ignore his feelings and chalk them up to simple jealousy, or is there something else far more dangerous about this Brendan MacArthur that Dulcie and Nick have yet to discover?

If you would like to read the Dulcie Chambers Mysteries please visit the author's website (kerryjcharles.com) for more information or request copies at your local bookstore or library. Ebook versions are also available from major suppliers online.

Reviews from thoughtful readers are always welcome on any website or media outlet. Thank you!

ABOUT THE AUTHOR

Kerry J Charles has worked as a researcher, writer, and editor for *National Geographic*, the Smithsonian Institution, Harvard University and several major textbook publishers. She holds four degrees including a Masters in Geospatial Engineering and a Masters in Art History from Harvard University. She has carried out research in many of the world's art museums as a freelance writer and scholar.

A swimmer, scuba diver, golfer, and boating enthusiast, Charles enjoys seeing the world from above and below sea level as well as from the tee box. Her life experiences inspire her writing and she is always seeking out new travels and adventures. She returned to her roots in coastal Maine while writing the Dulcie Chambers Mysteries.

Made in United States
Orlando, FL
15 July 2022

19785933R00152